The Duke's Heir

A Traditional Regency Romance

Mary Kingswood

Sutors Publishing

Published by Sutors Publishing

ISBN: 978-1-912167-63-0 (paperback)

v1

Cover design by: Shayne Rutherford of Darkmoon Graphics

Author's note:

this book is written using historic British terminology, so *saloon* instead of *salon*, *chaperon* instead of *chaperone* and so on. I follow Jane Austen's example and refer to a group of sisters as the Miss Wintertons.

Contents

About the book

The duke, his heir and a young lady who looks oddly familiar… just who is sending seemingly random strangers to the duke?

Mr Richard Merrington, country gentleman, has lived in the shadow of the Duke of Brinshire for his whole life. Now the duke's last son has died and Richard is summoned to Staineybank to take his place as the duke's heir. His comfortable life of obscurity is at an end, and his first duty is to marry. The noble ladies on offer leave him cold, so what is he to do?

Miss Rowena Holt has been left impoverished by her father's death, and must seek work as a governess or companion. It's a dispiriting prospect, but when a letter arrives inviting her to the Duke of Brinshire's house, it seems her fortunes have taken a turn for the better. But when she arrives, the residents react with shock…

This is a complete story with a happy ever after. A traditional Regency romance, drawing room rather than bedroom. Prequel to a 6 book series.

About the series*:*

Book 0: The Duke's Heir *(a novella prequel)*

Book 1: The Duke's Architect

Book 2: The Duke's Portraitist

Book 3: The Duke's Gardener

Book 4: The Duke's Steward

Book 5: The Duke's Librarian

Book 6: The Duke's Enemy

Want to be the first to hear about new releases? Sign up for my mailing list at https://marykingswood.co.uk.

The Duke's Household: Staineybank, Brinshire

Richard, 7th Duke of Brinshire

His family:

Lily nee Willaston, his duchess

Hester Merrington, his 'cousin'

His heir and family:

Richard Merrington, his heir

Mrs Roland Merrington (Cora), Richard's widowed mother

Richard's sisters:

Miss Charlotte Merrington

Miss Augusta Merrington

Miss Maria Merrington

Miss Sophia Merrington

His guests:

Rowena Holt, an unemployed governess

Mrs Henry Hastings (Georgie), the widowed companion to Rowena

His employees:

James Hammond, his secretary/memoirist

Mr Hammond Senior, his former secretary

Mr George Pyott, the comptroller

Mr William Godley, the chaplain

His servants:

Froggett, butler; Henry, Robert, footmen

Allen, Lily's lady's maid

Ben Lovell, the gamekeeper

1: The Heir

Staineybank, Brinshire: June

The Duke of Brinshire stared out of the windows at the incessant rain.

"Fitting weather for a funeral," he said. "Dear Lord, does it never stop?"

"There is no weather fitting for a burial," Lord Browning said from his seat by the library fire. "Sunshine is too mocking and rain too dreary. Come and sit down, Richard. Will you not give me your instructions?"

The duke turned to face him, without leaving his post by the window. "Three wives, Charles, *three*, and not a single living child. Not one. They did their best, and so did I, but it was not to be. But this last one... six years! Longer than any of the others, and a healthy boy, yet taken from us just the same. God has His reasons, I know, but we mortals struggle to understand them. I should have liked a child of my own blood to comfort my declining years. Just one. Still, we had this one for six years, and he was a great joy to us both, while he lived. Such a happy child, like his mother."

"How is her grace?" Charles said.

"Distraught, of course. Not that I have seen her since... since she put on her blacks. She keeps to her own apartments, but my people give me reports. She thinks me heartless, I dare say, to show no sign of grief, but I have buried too many over the years. Four sons who survived long enough to be baptised with my name. Four Richards. Four Marquesses of Losseter. Four graves in the churchyard, to set alongside all the others, and in all these long years, only one burial ever made me weep."

"Caroline. Your first duchess."

The duke nodded slowly. "So young! She died far too young. I swore then I would never fall in love again, and I have held to that vow. Jane... well, perhaps I went too far to the other extreme with her, but Lily... yes, Froggett, what is it?"

The butler coughed apologetically. "Mr Willaston begs the favour of a few words with your grace, if your grace can graciously spare him a little of your valuable time."

The duke sighed, but Charles chuckled, for that was probably a direct quotation.

"Yes, show him in, Froggett. Charles, you should not laugh at the poor man."

"I know, but he is such a ridiculous specimen. Are you so terrifying? Is he such a milksop that he must wilt like last week's lettuce before you? You are his son-in-law, after all."

But Mr Willaston of Elmhall in Cheshire was not a man accustomed to dealing with dukes. Only a mildly important man, even in his own county, he had never recovered from the shock of his pretty eldest daughter becoming a duchess. He crept into the room behind Froggett, and had bowed three times before the butler had finished announcing him.

"Ah, Willaston," the duke said. "Come in, come in. A glass of something?"

"Er... no... nothing, thank you, your grace."

"And how is Lily today?"

"Distressed... very distressed. Naturally. My poor daughter... such a tragedy... your grace—"

"You want to know what I intend for her, I imagine," the duke said gently.

"Well... it is... she would..."

"Of course," the duke said, for all the world as if Willaston were making any sense at all. "You may tell your daughter that I hold to the agreement that was made when we married. One son, that was all I asked of her, and she has fulfilled all my expectations in that regard."

Willaston exhaled a long, slow breath. "Ah..."

"Indeed, she exceeded them, for she stayed here with the boy, and he had the comfort of his mother's love for the whole of his short life. I shall always be grateful to her for that, for I know how she hates this place. And she brightened the life of an old man immeasurably. But she is free, now. She will always have a home here, if she wishes it, and the London house is available to her whenever she cares to use it, but if she wants an establishment of her own, that can be arranged."

"I think, your grace, if it would not incommode your grace excessively, Lily would like to return to her family home."

"Cheshire, then. By all means."

"We can squeeze her in at Elmhall, you know."

"Squeeze her in?" the duke said, straightening his back a little. "The Duchess of Brinshire is not to be *squeezed in*, Willaston. She will have an establishment worthy of her exalted rank, and a suitable number of servants, carriages, and so forth. Then *you* may squeeze in with *her*, eh?"

"Yes, your grace. Of course, your grace." He was bowing again, the sort of bow that signalled a man desperate to escape the interview.

"Well, off you go and tell her," the duke said, and Willaston, still bowing, reversed himself out of the room as if the duke were royalty.

Charles chuckled again, and shook his head. "I cannot imagine how you put up with him, Richard."

"He is seldom here, that is the only reason."

"Are you truly going to let her go? She is only six and twenty, and you know what will be said if she moves out — that you are in your dotage, and no longer capable of siring a child on her."

The duke shrugged. "Let the world say what it will, Charles. I no longer care. I am perfectly capable, but I have not the heart to subject that poor child to the amatory scrabblings of a man fifty years her senior. She deserves a better fate. Hester said it was undignified, and she was right, as usual. I have been trying to get an heir of my own blood for half a century, my friend. Enough! I am done with it."

"Then you will send for your cousin?"

"Second cousin, is he not?"

"Once removed."

"Tell me of him, Charles, for I know you have been watching him for me, just in case."

"What do you wish to know?"

"Only the basics."

"Well, then, he is five and twenty, a pleasant young man, by all accounts."

"A gentleman?"

"Certainly, although... not wealthy. His father died when he was twelve, mother not remarried. No school or university. He was tutored by the local parson, seemingly. His father's estate is rented out now, and he lives with his mother in a house in Norwich. He is... artistic, apparently."

The duke pulled a face. "He sounds a namby-pamby sort of fellow. Married?"

"No."

"Betrothed?"

"Not that I heard."

"And he knows?"

"He has been informed of your son's death, but if you truly intend to discontinue your efforts to produce an heir of your body, then this young man will be the next Duke of Brinshire, and I most strongly urge you to bring him here, so that he may grow accustomed to the honours and responsibilities which will one day fall to his lot. Including the necessity to sire the next heir."

"Hmpf." The duke paced across the room and back again. "What is his name, this artistic boy?"

Charles laughed. "Richard."

The duke gave a bark of laughter. "Let us hope the name brings him better fortune than his predecessors. Richard Merrington. Yes, he must live here now. I shall grow accustomed to him, I dare say. Let Hammond have the direction and I shall write to him."

***

Richard Merrington was not above average in height, but he towered over the diminutive lady quivering with indignation before him. "Well, madam? Will you explain why this bill for gowns was presented to me?"

"Now, Richard, you must not be in a dudgeon about such a trivial amount — only twenty pounds and—"

"Twenty pounds, four shillings and sixpence, and it would not matter if it were twenty shillings or twenty farthings, Mother. You must stay within your allowance. Why were you buying silk, anyway? What is wrong with cotton?"

"Oh, but Sophia looks so well in silk, and although we are not in full mourning for your cousin, we must mark the event with due propriety, soberly clad. Your sisters must present a suitable appearance to the world now that you are to be a duke, you know."

"But I am not a duke yet, nor do I have the income of a duke," Richard said tersely. "His grace may live for another twenty years, for all we know, or he may yet produce another son. We must not exceed our income, for that way lies ruination. How many times must I say this to you?"

"It is hard indeed to have my only son quibble over such trifling sums. Your father was not so unfeeling."

Richard sighed. "It is not unfeeling to insist that we live within our means, Mother. You and the girls consume half my income as it is, and I will not go into debt to drape Sophia in silk. If she is so fond of expensive gowns, she has my blessing to marry any rich man of her choosing, but she will not get them from me. I shall pay this bill, but your allowance for next quarter will be reduced accordingly, and I will tell this..." He scanned the bill. "...this Madame Alfonse that I shall pay no more of your debts, and she must apply to you for settlement in the future."

"Thank you, dearest," she said meekly, leaving him with the feeling that she had bested him in some way he could not quite fathom.

Sometimes he felt like a lodger in his own house, for with four unmarried sisters to support, as well as his widowed mother, he was very much outnumbered. The ladies ruled the household as they pleased, and he was obliged to fall in with their schemes. Only where money was concerned could he be said to have the upper hand, for he held the purse strings and he was quite determined to be beforehand with the world. To that end, as soon as he had come of age and wrested control of his affairs from his trustees, he had caused his estate of Leahollow to be leased out, and had removed his family to Norwich. If he also hoped this would provide his sisters with a better choice of husbands than rural Norfolk, and thereby relieve him of some part of the drain on his income, he kept this thought to himself. This was just as well, for the ladies had disappointed him and continued to live under his roof and clothe themselves at his expense, and he supposed now that they would always do so, since they were older than he was and approaching the status of settled spinsterhood.

He was adding the details of the bill to his accounts when John the footman crept in. One of the disadvantages of the move to Norwich was the more rapid turnover in servants. Footmen, in particular, seldom stayed for more than a six-month before finding themselves a more prestigious post. John had been with them for no more than three weeks, and already he was delegated to deliver the mail to Richard. That should, more properly, have been the job of Shackell, the butler, but he expressed his disgust with the move from a proper gentleman's estate to a much smaller town house by refusing to undertake such trivial tasks. Richard suspected that he only stayed on because he knew that his master was heir to a dukedom.

"Thank you, John," Richard said, looking with disfavour on the great mound of letters on the salver, most boasting florid female hands and smelling of some unearthly perfume. More invitations, no doubt. There had been a noticeable increase in the popularity of the Merrington family since the sad announcement in the important newspapers of the death of the Duke of Brinshire's only son and heir.

Methodically, he sorted through the letters, most being for his mother, a smattering for one or other of the girls, and only a few, addressed in sober male lettering, to him. These he extracted from the heap, gave the salver back to John to be placed on the hall table for the ladies to see, and began to open his own mail. It was the third letter that gave him pause.

'To Mr Richard Merrington, Winterdale House, Norwich. Sir, His Grace the Duke of Brinshire has instructed me to write to you in the following terms, that you are invited to present yourself at Staineybank, near Brinchester in the county of Brinshire at your earliest convenience. Respectfully yours, James Hammond, Secretary to His Grace.'

Staineybank! He was to meet the duke at last, so perhaps his grace had finally given up all hope of a son of his own. There was no prospect now of escaping his fate. He would be the next Duke of Brinshire, whether he liked it or not, and in his heart he very much disliked it. His life in Norwich was greatly to his taste, for here he had a numerous acquaintance, could dine out five nights out of seven if he so chose, and he had his little hobby to occupy his hands and his mind, and bring in a useful income, as well. He could not imagine that the duke would approve of his heir involving himself in any paid employment.

He folded the letter neatly away, and placed it in his waistcoat pocket, but wherever he went that day, whatever tasks he undertook, that letter burned in his mind like a coal straight from the fire.

It was almost the dinner hour before he had an opportunity to inform the ladies of the matter. They had all gathered in the drawing room, and he was handing round the customary small glasses of sherry before he said, "I shall be going away tomorrow for a while."

"Going away? But where?" his mother said. "Have you forgotten the Wiltshires' dinner on Saturday?"

"I have not forgotten it, but I shall have to cry off. I have been summoned to Staineybank."

The ladies all cried out at this stupendous news.

"But you cannot possibly go away and leave us," his mother said firmly. "Five ladies alone in the house, with no male to protect us? It is not to be thought of. We shall come with you."

"You are not invited, Mother, and I cannot refuse to go. It is my duty."

"Do you owe no duty to your poor widowed mother? Or your unmarried sisters? Are we less worthy of your duty than a man who has ignored you for your entire life? He has taken not one whit of notice of you all these years, but now that he decides on a whim to take you up, we are to be neglected, I suppose."

"It is too bad of you, Richard," Charlotte said.

"I suppose you will take the carriage and horses, and we shall be unable to go anywhere," Augusta said.

"You promised to take us to the theatre, too," Maria said.

"And how shall we go to the assembly next week with no man to escort us?" Sophia said.

"Of course, if his grace were to invite all of us..." his mother said, and his sisters nodded their heads.

"That would be quite a different case," Charlotte said.

"Oh yes, it would put a different complexion on it altogether," Augusta said.

Richard sighed. "Very well, but I cannot directly solicit an invitation."

"You can subtly hint at it, however," his mother said, with a smug smile. "Such a pity the ladies will not be able to accompany me... or something of the sort. You will know just how to frame it."

That brought another sigh. "I will do my best."

The next morning, after a sleepless night spent wondering just how one subtly induced an elderly duke to issue an invitation to five ladies of no interest to him, he took up his pen.

'To the Most Noble the Duke of Brinshire, Staineybank, near Brinchester, Brinshire. My Lord Duke, I thank you for your very kind invitation to attend you at Staineybank, but I cannot leave my mother and sisters alone at this present. Your grace's most obedient servant, Richard Merrington.'

Five days later, a second letter arrived.

'To Mr Richard Merrington, Winterdale House, Norwich. Sir, His Grace the Duke of Brinshire has instructed me to inform you that you may bring your mother and sisters as well. Respectfully yours, James Hammond, Secretary to His Grace.'

The ladies burst into excited chattering, all their previous objections instantly overcome.

"Will he pay us an allowance?" Charlotte said.

"I shall be able to ride again," Augusta said with satisfaction.

"There is bound to be a library," Maria said.

"Will there be a ballroom?" Sophia said.

Their mother laughed and clapped her hands with glee. "Oh, how *clever* of you to persuade him to invite all of us, Richard. Now we are bound to find good husbands for all the girls. Do you think he will put up dowries for them?"

Richard sighed. Only an hour, perhaps an hour and a half, and they would leave him alone with the port, and after that he could plead that he had letters to write. At least with so many women in the house, they could always get up a four for whist if they wanted it, and he could find something more interesting to do with his evenings.

But at Staineybank, who knew how he would be expected to pass the time? His life was changing, and not at all for the better.

***

Miss Rowena Holt sighed, and leaned back in her chair, eyes closed, the day's letters still clutched in her hand.

"Anything promising?" her friend said, without looking up from the chemise she was stitching.

"Two more refusals, and neither of them franked. At this rate, my meagre savings will be entirely consumed by postage costs."

"I do think it's too bad of these people, when you send your letters to them paid in advance, that they don't have the courtesy to do the same," Georgie said. "Still, something is bound to turn up soon. Wasn't there a third letter?"

"There was. Take a look at it and tell me what you make of it."

Georgie carefully secured her needle, then took the proffered letter, reading it aloud. "'*To Miss Rowena Holt, Oakfordham Cottage, near Oxford. Madam, if you would care to present yourself at Staineybank, Brinshire, you will discover something to your material advantage. A carriage will collect you at nine in the morning of the 14th inst. All travelling costs will be defrayed. You may wish to bring a travelling companion. Respectfully yours, A Goodenough (attorney at law), Castle Street, Brinchester'* Well! That is something, indeed. Staineybank… I don't recall you mentioning a Staineybank."

"It is not one of the places to which I applied," Rowena said, puzzled. "I have never heard of it. Where is Brinshire? Somewhere to the north and west of here… Shropshire, Staffordshire… around there."

"Mr Clark has a copy of Paterson, so we can look up Staineybank in that. He'll be home just now for his dinner. Shall I…?"

"No, let us both go," Rowena said. "But Georgie, this is a very odd thing. All these refusals, and now I get a positive response from a place I did not even apply to."

"I expect they've heard of your situation from someone else. That's how it works with these families, Rowena. If Lady A has no need of a governess at present, but she knows that Lady B is looking for someone, then she'll tell her about you. That's what has happened, you may be sure. Come, dear, let's apply to Mr Clark for a sight of Paterson."

Mr Clark, an elderly attorney who lodged in the cottage next door with the widowed Mrs Burnley, was delighted to look up Staineybank in his elderly and well-thumbed copy of Paterson's Itinerary.

"My goodness! Look at this, Miss Holt, Mrs Hastings. *'Staineybank, the magnificent seat of the Duke of Brinshire… august and noble appearance… from wing to wing more than 300 feet… pillars, porticoes, pediments…'* Heavens above! The library has over ten thousand volumes! Just imagine it! *'Spacious and lofty apartments… superlatively rich… paintings by the first masters… extensive and delightful gardens'.* My dear Miss Holt, I congratulate you most sincerely. A duke! I do not suppose you ever dared to hope for such a lofty position. But we must go at once to the rectory, for Mr Childs has a recent peerage. We must find out how many children this duke has."

At the rectory, the elderly Mr Childs excitedly pulled out his copy of the peerage. "Oh. Only one child, a boy of... he must be six now. Just the age to need a governess."

"But only for a year or two, until he will need a tutor for Latin and Greek, and then school," Rowena said disappointedly. "Still, it would be better than nothing, and a good reference for when I have to move on."

It was white haired Miss Childs who sank this pleasant dream, moving across to the table where sat a pile of recent newspapers. "But was it not the Duke of Brinshire...? I am sure I read it in the *Gazette*... Yes, here it is. *'All England mourns with the Duke and Duchess of Brinshire, suffering with noble dignity the recent tragic demise of their only child, the Marquess of Losseter, at the age of just six years.'* You see? The boy is dead."

"Then why on earth am I summoned to Staineybank?" Rowena said, bewildered.

2: Staineybank

Richard could not leave Norwich without a visit to his estate of Leahollow, just a few miles outside the city, which was leased to a merchant and his family. Leaving the ladies in a twitter of excitement to organise packing, with a reminder to be sure to take plenty of black gowns, since the duke was in mourning, he rode at an easy pace through several small villages before turning in at the gates. Old Marler, the former gamekeeper, limped out of the lodge as fast as his creaking legs would allow to bow low in respect.

The drive was free of weeds, he noted, and the gardens in excellent order. His tenants were taking good care of the place. At the house, the butler admitted him at once and he passed a pleasant hour with the merchant, discussing the state of the farms and the prospects for the harvest. A few minutes with the ladies of the household as a courtesy, and he was away again, collecting his horse directly from the stables, and riding to the stretch of woodland where his bailiff was believed to be that day. After another favourable report, he felt comfortable setting off for the real object of his day, the small village of Lingwood Green in the parish of St Mark's, just a mile away.

There in the vicarage resided the man to whom he owed his entire education. Dr Ingleton was a man of some learning, who had supplemented his modest stipend by tutoring boys intended for Eton or Harrow. Richard had wondered about Eton, too, and Oxford thereafter, but his father having died at a young age, he had declared his preference to stay at home and continue his lessons with the vicar, and his fond mama had made no demur to this pleasant scheme. A fortunate inheritance had seen Dr Ingleton freed from any pecuniary shortfall, but he had continued to teach Richard until he reached his majority and moved away from Leahollow.

Even now, Richard regularly made the journey to Lingwood Green, partly to keep a watchful eye on Leahollow, but mainly to talk to his tutor and mentor.

Joe Ingleton was delighted to see him, as always. He was not yet fifty, but a slightly stooped posture and a good sprinkling of grey about the temples made him look older than his years. He rarely left the village now, but he had friends and relations scattered all over the country and was always very well informed on the latest *on-dits.* His hobby was to compile family trees for the kingdom's most prominent families, and every surface in his parlour was piled high with vast sheets of paper covered in spiders' webs of connections and lines of descent. He cheerfully cleared space on a table near the fire, brought out a very decent claret and ordered a light repast from the kitchen. The two then settled themselves in their usual chairs, glasses in hand.

"So the Brinshire boy is dead," Joe said. "The poor duke! How he must feel it, and this one lasted longer than any of the others."

"Did he?" Richard said, startled. "I did not know that."

"Six years. The first son lasted three years, but the second and third under two. One of the daughters survived for five years. Poor man! He must wonder what he has to do to get an heir."

"You are very well informed," Richard said. "You have the family tree in good order, I suppose."

"Well, naturally, given its importance to you, Richard. I wonder if he will try again. The present duchess is still very young."

"I suspect not," Richard said. "I am sent for."

"Ah." Joe sipped his claret thoughtfully. "Quite a disruption for you."

Richard sighed. "It is the last thing I want, as you know. My life is precisely how I want it. At least... I should be happier if the girls were settled, but they show no inclination towards matrimony. They are so expensive, you have no idea."

Joe laughed. "That will hardly be a consideration now, surely? As the acknowledged heir presumptive, you will be very much in funds henceforth. His grace is one of the richest men in the kingdom."

"Is he?"

That brought another spurt of laughter. "You know nothing about him, do you? I should have thought you would have wanted to know everything about your inheritance."

"I *do* know everything about my inheritance," Richard said stiffly. "Leahollow is my inheritance, and I assure you, I know it intimately. But Staineybank? I have always hoped I would never need to know it. I decided a long time ago that I would not even think about the dukedom until the day that a troop of lawyers with black armbands arrive on the doorstep to inform me that I am the new Duke of Brinshire. And I devoutly hoped that day would never come. Even now, I hope to have a few years yet. How old is he, Joe?"

"Seventy-six, and still hale, by all I hear. You will have time to grow accustomed to the idea."

Richard groaned. "I wish I need not! What am I to do? My comfortable life is over."

"You know the answer to that perfectly well — your duty. If the duke has sent for you, then your future is Staineybank, and Leahollow will become just another of the duke's lesser holdings."

Richard rose and walked abstractedly across the room to the window, with its fine view of the church.

"You do realise the first duty that will be expected of you?" Joe said. "You will be required to marry."

"What?" Richard spun round in horror, and Joe burst out laughing.

"Oh, if you could see your face! But it will be a matter of some urgency, Richard, since there is no other heir in sight. Surely you want to marry?"

"Oh, eventually. I always thought... once the girls were off my hands, I could look about me for an amenable girl. But not yet, surely! I am only twenty-five."

"The perfect age, I should have said, and if you are truly the heir presumptive, you will have the daughters of the nobility falling over themselves to attract your attention."

Richard groaned. "Oh, no! The season... balls... Almack's! My dear friend, how am I to survive it?"

Joe chuckled. "You may find that the duke has someone in mind for you."

"Which would be even worse — an arranged match. What a nightmare! Joe, if it all gets too much I may write to you even more than usual. You will not mind that, I hope?"

"Quite the reverse, dear boy. I want to hear everything. No detail is too trivial to interest me. After all, I have devoted much of my life to tracing the connections between the houses of the nobility. I look forward to your reports avidly."

***

The trunks were packed, the Norwich house was shuttered and closed up, the knocker removed, and a small procession of carriages wended its slow way from Norfolk to Brinshire. The ladies were in high feather, chattering endlessly in a mindless deluge of unfounded speculation. At the first change of horses, Richard decamped to share the luggage wagon with his valet, leaving his mother and the two maids in the small town coach, and his sisters in the more capacious travelling carriage. They grumbled, of course. They grumbled about everything.

"If you wish me to survive three days on the road with my sanity intact, I must have quietude," he said firmly.

There was no avoiding them at the post houses where they stayed overnight, but he could at least retreat to his own room when the feminine element became overwhelming. He had never bemoaned his lot in having so many sisters, although he wondered often just why they had never married. One unmarried sister he might have borne with equanimity as company for his mother, but four of them was overpowering when not one of them had a rational thought in her head. If but one would marry, then one or two of the others could be dispatched to inflict themselves on her poor husband, but despite the unflagging interest in gowns and bonnets and balls and society in general, not one had, so far as he knew, received even one offer. They were not antidotes, and were pleasant enough company in ones and twos, he supposed, yet somehow they had never taken. And now they were quite sure that the duke's protection would bring them the husbands they so obviously wanted.

Perhaps it would, who could tell? The society in Brinshire would be different, that much was certain. Not the easy society he was used to, with gentle card parties, musical evenings and, very occasionally, when it could not be avoided, a ball. A duke must move in very different society, he supposed. Well, he would find out soon enough, and perhaps the duke would not require him to stay. Perhaps this was merely an introductory visit, after which he could return to Norwich and normality again. That was a cheering thought.

Brinshire proved to be a pleasant county, not so flat as Norfolk, and with many productive farms. The houses were built of a pleasing red stone or else of brick, with a solid, substantial air to them, and although the children ran barefoot amongst the chickens, that was no different from Norfolk. They passed through the prosperous town of Brinchester and then, only three or four miles beyond it, a small village bordered by the well-kept walls of Staineybank.

A vast ceremonial arch marked the entrance, the high wrought-iron gates closed, but the gatekeeper exchanged a few words with the postilions and the gates slowly swung open. They rolled through, and proceeded up a short drive, the house gradually coming into view. At first, they saw only the nearest end of the building, but as the drive swept round to the front, they could see the full majesty of the house. Richard's eyes widened.

"Three hundred and fifty feet from end to end, and three storeys," Weston said. "Do you think they will be able to squeeze us all in, sir?"

Richard laughed. "I think they might just manage it. Great heavens! So big!"

"The right size for a duke, wouldn't you say, sir?"

Richard had no need to answer, for they drew up before a central projecting wing, where wide stone steps were rapidly being traversed by footmen, and a pair of superior beings descended who must be the butler and housekeeper.

As soon as Richard stepped from the carriage, the butler moved forward. "Mr Merrington? Welcome to Staineybank, sir. I am Froggett, butler here, and this is Miss Hester Merrington."

Not the housekeeper, then, although she dressed exactly like one, and was the right age, too. Richard guessed her to be somewhat above forty.

"Pray call me Cousin Hester," she said in a soft voice. "It's close enough. Oh!" She caught sight of Richard's sisters, descending from their carriage in a flutter of excitement. "Oh dear. We had not expected so many ladies."

"My sisters can double up, if you are short of bedrooms," he said blandly.

She caught his eye, and laughed. "Oh, we can find room for you all, but we've only prepared four bedrooms just now. But if the Miss Merringtons would be so good as to share two rooms just for tonight, we can arrange matters for greater comfort tomorrow. Mrs Merrington, welcome to Staineybank, and all the Miss Merringtons. So pleased... welcome, welcome. Would you care to come inside? I am Hester Merrington, but everyone calls me Cousin Hester. Pray do not trouble yourself about the luggage, Froggett will see to it. This is the Marble Hall, Mrs Merrington. The stairs are this way if you would be so good as to follow me."

Richard ambled along in their wake, craning his neck to see the painted ceiling far above, passing great marble pillars that made him feel like a caterpillar crawling about in a giant forest made of stone. It was curiously unsettling.

Wide stairs led to an upper floor, one sumptuously appointed chamber leading to another, until they arrived at a pair of double doors standing open.

"We thought the Queen's Suite would suit you best," Cousin Hester said. "A sitting room here, where you can be together as a family when you want to be private, and four bedrooms off it. There is a smaller stair just through that door. Mr Merrington? Ah, there you are. I thought this room for you."

It was a beautiful room, he had to admit, with elegant furnishings of a somewhat old-fashioned type, and perhaps six times the size of his room at Norwich. Even at Leahollow, he had not been so commodiously accommodated. But it would not do.

"The ladies may have these rooms," he said. "I should like a room somewhere else."

"Richard, what is wrong with this room?" his mother said, gazing around it.

"Nothing, but you will have more space for your gowns and so forth if you have a spare room here. There is no need for us to be on top of each other like this, not in such a big house."

"But—"

"Let me show you some other rooms," Cousin Hester said, hastily, seeing that a family argument was brewing.

Richard let him lead her out of the suite, where his mother was distracted by the arrival of the first of their boxes, and back through the same succession of chambers.

"What sort of room had you in mind, Mr Merrington?" Cousin Hester said, a thread of amusement in her tone.

"I do not care about the room, so long as it is as far as possible from my sisters," he murmured.

She laughed out loud at that. "Let me show you the Losseter suite, then."

The Losseter suite was comprised of three rooms, a vast bedchamber, an only marginally smaller dressing room and an even larger room that could be described as a sitting room or study. The furniture was shrouded in holland covers, but Cousin Hester whisked them off to show him the solid furniture beneath, and he was satisfied.

"This will do very well, Cousin Hester. If it is not too intrusive, might I enquire as to the precise nature of your cousinship? For I am a cousin myself, and take an interest in such things."

She chuckled. "Niece to his grace, to be precise, but the wrong side of the blanket by way of his grace's younger brother, Lord Rupert. Cousin covers a multitude of sins, Mr Merrington."

"So it does, but since I am to call you Cousin Hester, I do not see why you should not call me Cousin Richard."

"Thank you!" Her thin face went a little pink. "You are very good but his grace may have other ideas as to how you should be addressed by the lower orders."

"But you are family," he said gently. "Of an irregular nature, perhaps, but you bear the Merrington name."

"I am acknowledged, perhaps, and even tolerated, so long as I make myself useful," she said, with a hint of waspishness, "but I am not and never will be accepted as family, Mr Merrington. Now this window overlooks the shrubbery, and from this one, there is a fine view over the *parterre,*" she added, throwing open one shutter after another.

"I do not care about the view," he murmured, making her laugh again.

"Just the distance from your sisters, yes. Understood. Ah, Froggett, there you are. Mr Merrington's luggage may be brought in here, and inform his man of the change of rooms. Also, we shall need a couple of housemaids to remove these covers, and we may require footmen to shift furniture about."

"No need for furniture shifting," Richard said. "Let us see if I shall be staying long enough to make that worthwhile."

Her eyebrows rose, and when Froggett had left, she said, "You plan to leave?"

"I have no plan at all. I have been summoned, and so I have come, but I wait to hear his grace's plan for me."

"Ah. I see. Well—"

The door flew open and an elderly man strode in. He was not greatly above the average in height, but had an imposing presence, and Richard did not doubt that this was the duke himself.

"What is going on? Hester, what are you doing in here?" he said, bushy eyebrows lowered. He stared at Richard. "Who the devil are you?"

"Richard Merrington, your grace," he said, executing a low bow.

"Ha! Here already? I did not expect you until tomorrow. Well, you are not an imposing specimen, are you? Scrawny little thing. How old are you?"

"Twenty-five, sir."

"Hmm." He raked Richard from head to toe and then back again. "Hester, I thought we agreed on the Queen's suite?"

"So we did, your grace, but Mr Merrington preferred to be away from his family. It leaves a little more room for his mother and four sisters," she added carefully.

"Four! Good God, man! And you are the only son?"

"I am, sir."

"Are they older or younger than you?"

"All older. All unmarried."

The duke grunted, and then slowly began to laugh. "No wonder you wanted to be away from them. Well, this is the appropriate place for you, I suppose. The Losseter suite is intended for the Marquess of Losseter — the heir, you see. Not been used for years now, but... yes, it is fitting for you to have it. You may do what you will with it. Redecorate, refurnish, whatever you need to make you comfortable. It will be your home for some time, for I have no intention of turning up my toes just yet. Hester will look after you. We dine at five sharp. Meet in the White Drawing Room at half past four, and knee breeches, mind. None of this new-fangled idea of trousers as evening wear. I cannot abide the things. And be on time. I cannot abide unpunctuality."

"Very good, your grace."

"Hmm. And none of this *'your grace'* business. You are family, after all, so you call me *'Duke'*. Understood?"

"Yes, Duke."

"Hmpf. We will knock you into shape eventually, I suppose. Until this evening, then."

And he was gone, leaving Richard bemused and despondent in equal measure. At least one question was answered — he was expected to live at Staineybank from now on. This was his future, whether he liked it or not.

3: On The Road From Oxford

Richard arrived in the White Drawing Room, aided by a helpful footman, precisely as the clock struck the half hour. Weston had been in a great lather, quite overwhelmed by the splendour of the ducal household, and fumbled this garment or that so many times that Richard had to gently reprove him. He had remembered to wear black, and he found his mother and all his sisters were already there, also arrayed in their best blacks for the occasion.

Charlotte and Augusta were wandering about the room, another overly ornate apartment, admiring the various artworks on the walls and the busts and vases scattered about. Maria had inevitably found the single shelf of books in a corner, while Sophia was leafing through the music beside the pianoforte. Mother sat primly on a gilded chair looking rather like a queen on her throne.

"Are you comfortably situated with your rooms, Mother?" he said, pulling up another chair. "Do you have everything you need?"

"Oh yes. In a house like this, no detail would be overlooked. I did not expect to find any deficiency, and I have not. What about you?"

"I find myself in the heir's apartments," he said with a rueful smile. "The Losseter Suite. I am authorised to make whatever changes I wish, so it seems that I, at least, am expected to stay."

She raised delicately arched eyebrows. "Naturally you will stay, and we shall stay with you. I cannot abandon my only son."

"This is not my house, Mother. The duke's wishes must prevail."

She tittered. "I think, Richard, that as the *future* duke, your wishes might also carry some weight."

"Hardly, Mother, and even if it were so, I am not about to start playing the great lord and issuing peremptory orders. If I had been born and raised here, then perhaps, but at present I am too new to Staineybank. We must all feel our way into this new life. Ah, the duke."

He strode in, his gaze sweeping the room, lingering momentarily on Richard and his mother, then taking in the four girls. That caused the eyebrows to lower ominously. However, he stepped towards Richard first.

"On time, I see. Good. Pray introduce me, boy."

"This is my mother, Duke, Mrs Roland Merrington, and my sisters..." He paused as they lined up in the correct order. This is my eldest sister, Charlotte, then Augusta, Maria and Sophia. His Grace the Duke of Brinshire."

"Hmpf." The brows lowered even more. "How old are you?" he said to Charlotte.

"I am thirty years of age, your grace."

"And still unmarried. None of you is married? Betrothed?" They all shook their heads dolefully. He turned to Richard. "You will have trouble getting them off your hands now, boy. Well now, you are all welcome to Staineybank. I hope you enjoy your stay here, and will return home satisfied that your brother is in good hands. Ah, here is Hester now, and the others. I shall leave her to introduce you."

Richard had to suppress a grin at the chagrin on the ladies' faces at this summary dismissal. They were not, then, expected to stay, and he could not be sorry for it.

Cousin Hester introduced the three men who had followed her into the room. Mr Hammond, a man of about Richard's own age with a ready smile and knowing eyes, was the duke's secretary and memoirist, currently engaged in tabulating his grace's diaries preparatory to the writing of a history of his travels and political experiences. Mr Pyott, a bluff, cheerful man of middle years, was the comptroller. The aptly named Mr Godley, a beanpole of a man of about thirty-five, was the chaplain, whose eyes gleamed at the sight of the Merrington sisters.

The footmen had handed round glasses of sherry to those who wished it, and Richard was industriously making polite conversation with Pyott, when there was a stir around the door. The duke, standing a little aside, looked up, and Richard was astonished to see a smile break out across his craggy features.

"Lily! My dear girl!"

Striding across the room, he halted before the prettiest little creature Richard had ever seen. She was dressed in deepest mourning, but that only served to enhance her beauty. He was conscious of a very reprehensible wish that his sisters, or even one sister, had been half so pretty, for then surely they would have married easily. And then, as it slowly dawned on him that the pretty creature was in fact the Duchess of Brinshire, that he, too, could marry someone like that, if he wanted.

The duke led her into the room on his arm. "Lily, my dear, this is my heir... another Richard, I regret to say. There have been too many of those."

His face clouded for a moment, and her eyes filled with tears, but then she rallied again. "I have wanted so much to meet you, Richard. Oh, may I call you that? And you must call me Lily, none of this *'your grace'* business, for it makes me feel so old. We are much the same age, are we not? Oh, and this is my sister, Miss Elinor Willaston."

Richard had not even noticed the plain, dumpy girl beside her, quite outshone by her lovely sister.

"Duchess," Richard said, bowing. "Miss Willaston. May I present to you my mother and sisters?"

"Oh, yes, please!" the duchess cried. "We have come out of seclusion to eat in company tonight precisely for that purpose. You cannot know how delightful it is to see so many young ladies here. I do not feel nearly so out of place. Pray introduce me at once."

Transferring her arm to Richard's, she made straight for the gaggle of ladies and Richard found himself immersed in an excitable discussion of fashions. The duke, who had followed them, exchanged an amused glance with him, and for the first time, Richard felt an affinity with this remote personage who held his future in his hands.

***

It was a strange evening, to be sure. The duchess drew all Richard's sisters away to the other end of the table, whence emanated a continuous chorus of feminine voices. He doubted that any of them ate at all.

At the duke's end of the table, Richard endured a catechism on his education and upbringing generally. Most of his information was received with no more than a grunt, but Richard could not and would not apologise for any deficiencies. He had never expected to inherit, and if the duke had been at all concerned at the possibility, he could have stepped in at any time to ensure that Richard had what he regarded as a more suitable education. Having ignored him for his entire life, he could hardly complain that Richard had not been raised to ducal standards.

Occasionally, the duke turned to Richard's mother on his other side, but he quickly wearied of her inconsequential chatter and effusive compliments, and turned back to Richard. The only relief came from Hammond, the secretary, who turned out to be a nephew of Joe Ingleton, Richard's tutor, so they both had happy memories to impart.

Sometimes, however, the duke fell silent, gazing down the table at his duchess, engrossed with her new friends. As the dessert was brought in, he turned to Richard's mother.

"Madam, I must congratulate you."

"Oh... how very kind, your grace. Um... for what, precisely?"

"Your daughters have achieved what I could not, in inducing the duchess to leave her apartments and join the world once more. She has been sadly grieved, naturally... her only child, and such a delightful boy. We had such hopes... but it was not to be, and my poor Lily was prostrate with grief. She could barely leave her bed. She wishes to go home to Cheshire to be nearer her family, and the agents are even now searching for a suitable house, but while she waits, she has been hiding in her apartment. But now, a little company of her own age and sex, and see how lively she is! She always has one or other of her sisters with her, but they never have this effect. Why, she has been smiling almost constantly, and I distinctly heard her laugh on three separate occasions. It warms my heart, madam, and so I congratulate you."

"Oh! Oh, thank you, indeed. I am sure my girls are only too happy—"

"Yes, yes, but they must stay, do you see? You must not whisk them away to Nottingham—"

"Norfolk."

"Nottingham, Norfolk... it is immaterial. They must stay, for Lily's sake, until she goes to Cheshire. Amongst her own people, she will repair her heart and recover her spirits. Such a charming girl, when she is in spirits, and quite brightened an old man's days, but she must go now wherever will make her happy. This house oppresses her, I think."

"Oh, yes, I can quite—"

"But until then, your daughters must stay here."

"Yes, your grace. Of course, your grace."

When the ladies withdrew, the five gentlemen gathered around the duke and the port.

"Well, boy, what do you think of us, eh? Do we pass muster?" And he chuckled, knowing that Richard could hardly answer such a question.

"I rather thought that I was the one being weighed up," Richard said mildly.

"And so you are, but you are judging us, as well, and sizing up your inheritance. What do you think of Staineybank, eh?"

"It is a very appropriate residence for a duke," he said, causing a ripple of amusement round the table. "As to sizing up my inheritance, I shall not be able to do that until I have sight of the accounts."

"Ha! You want to see the accounts, do you? Shall we let him, Pyott?"

"That is entirely a matter for your grace to determine."

"We shall see," the duke said, the eyebrows lowering again in an ominous fashion. "Let me see what you are made of, first of all, boy. Tomorrow you will ride with my head groom directly after breakfast, and in the afternoon you will take a gun out with my gamekeeper. They will report to me on where you need improvement. The day after, you will talk to the bailiff — he will show you about the estate and see how much you know of such matters. In the evening, there is an assembly in Brinchester. Hester will take you in, and report on your skills in that direction. Well? Anything to say, boy?"

"My sisters would enjoy the assembly, sir. Might I take them with me?"

"I shall only want to send one carriage, so you may take two of them with you."

"As you please, sir, but since we have our own carriage here, I would not wager a groat on my mother and the remaining two staying at home, if there is dancing to be had."

The duke gave a rumble of laughter. "They are a handful, your women, eh? Very well. On Sunday we attend divine service in the chapel here, and on Monday we will begin making plans for your marriage."

"I am to marry, am I?" Richard said.

"You are, and as soon as may be. Understand this, boy, the getting of an heir is now a matter of some importance. After you, the next heir is wildly unsuitable — an attorney, or some such. You at least have the air of a gentleman about you."

"Thank you, I am sure," Richard murmured.

"You dress tolerably well, and you are no dandy, which is all to the good. I cannot abide a dandy. Your manners are unexceptionable, I will say that for you, so however deficient your education in general, your mother did her duty in that regard. We will get you up to snuff, never fret, and maybe next spring I shall make the effort to go up to town and show you around, get you presented at court and into White's."

"I am already a member of White's, sir."

"Hmpf. One less thing to worry about. But I want you married before then, and setting about securing the succession. Hester has already started work on a list of suitable candidates, and once it becomes known that you will definitely inherit, there will not be the least difficulty."

Richard hesitated, but the question had to be asked, and answered unambiguously. "Shall I definitely inherit, Duke? The duchess is young still, and you are clearly as fit as a flea, so might there yet be a possibility that—?"

"No!" The dukes's voice was harsh. "God has seen fit to deny me a son of my body, and the time has come for me to accept His will. Perhaps if we tried I could get Lily with child again, but she deserves better than an old man like me. She has never been happy here, but she has done her duty, and now I shall let her go to be happy in whatever way she wishes until my death sets her free. So the obligation to produce the next heir falls to you, boy, and the sooner the better, understand?"

"Perfectly, but I must have some say in my choice of bride."

"*Must?*" The eyebrows became dangerously low.

"I must. I accept that she must be suitable for the position, and I will of course take your advice on that, but I cannot marry someone for whom I feel no affinity. I do not ask for love—"

"Just as well!"

"—but there must be some affection, of friendship, if nothing else. I ask only this, Duke. In every other respect, I will abide by your wishes absolutely, but my wife I must choose myself."

The duke only grunted.

***

Rowena and Georgie had packed their things into two small boxes and a couple of valises, had an early breakfast and were waiting, in their travelling pelisses and bonnets, ready to depart shortly before nine o'clock on the appointed day.

Now that the moment had come, Rowena was beginning to doubt the wisdom of simply stepping into an unknown carriage to be conveyed to an unknown destination.

"What if we are being kidnapped to be sold to slave traders?" she said to Georgie. "Or... or worse." Although she could not imagine what would be worse.

"It seems too elaborate a ploy for that. Slavers simply snatch people off the street, surely? And we're certainly not likely to be rushed to Gretna by fortune hunters."

"That is true enough," Rowena said, laughing. "But still... we know nothing of this Duke of Brinshire, except that he has no son in need of a governess."

"There may be other children — nephews and nieces, perhaps. Orphaned cousins. A duke's household is likely to be a large one."

"Oh, that is possible." Rowena brightened a little. "But still, not a word in the letter about children or needing a governess or anything of the sort, only that a carriage will be sent. Am I doing a very foolish thing, Georgie?"

"Let's see what the carriage looks like before we decide."

"We shall look very silly if no carriage arrives," Rowena said.

"The letter was quite specific," Georgie said. "Nine o'clock on the fourteenth, and this is— Wait! Do you hear that?" She rushed to the window. "A carriage! Is it stopping? It is! Our transport has arrived."

But she sounded surprised about it, all the same.

It was a remarkably commodious carriage, not a post chaise, with two pairs of horses and postilions, and another man on the box, who jumped down as soon as the wheels ceased moving. He was perhaps forty, soberly dressed in black, almost like a clergyman, but his demeanour was cheerful.

"Miss Rowena Holt?" he called out loudly, as they emerged from the front door. "How do you do, madam. I am Arthur Goodenough, the attorney. You had my letter, I take it? I can see you are all ready to depart. Excellent, excellent. And this is...?"

"Mrs Hastings. My travelling companion. You said I might bring someone..."

"Yes, yes, of course. It is a long journey, two days at least, if we suffer no mishaps, so you will want a friend with you. Might we go inside a moment to discuss the arrangements?"

"Of course."

They sat down again at the breakfast table that they had just left, and Mr Goodenough reached into a pocket. "My card," he said. "Now, firstly, I can tell you nothing about the reason for your journey for I do not know it. I am merely following orders from my client, to write to you and then to convey you to Staineybank."

"Is your client the Duke of Brinshire?"

"I cannot say, madam. Naturally, you will be nervous about putting yourselves in the hands of a complete stranger, so my client wished you to have a companion with you, to reassure you. There is also this." He rummaged in a pocket and produced a heavy purse. "One hundred guineas, to defray any incidental expenses, and as insurance, in case you should at any time have second thoughts about the journey. That amount is sufficient to enable you to return home at any time."

"Thank you," Rowena said faintly, grasping the purse tightly. So much money! She could not recall a time when she had ever had so much in her hand, even in the better days, although it seemed an excessive amount of money to hand over to a governess.

"Now, as to the journey itself, I shall travel on the box at all times, not in the carriage with you. We should only need one overnight stop, but I have arranged a private parlour for you — I shall eat in the common room — and your chamber will have a solid lock. I have only taken one room for you, since I presumed you would wish to share, but it is a large room, so you will not be cramped. Do you have any questions?"

Rather dazed, Rowena shook her head. "Georgie?"

Georgie smiled. "It's an adventure, isn't it? Shall we go?"

The journey was indeed an adventure, but of the very best sort. Having only occasionally travelled by public stage, and once, unforgettably, in a hired post chaise in a mad dash to Granny Holt's deathbed, to Rowena's mind the supplied carriage was luxurious indeed. With room for four inside, the two ladies, neither being large, had more than enough space to be comfortable. Georgie was small enough to curl up on one seat and sleep, if she wished, and although Rowena was too tall for such a position, there was ample room for her to stretch out. Mr Goodenough had thoughtfully provided several rugs, in case of draughts, and a hamper of food and drink to sustain them on the journey, although they had prudently brought food of their own.

Georgie instantly dived into the hamper, exclaiming in delight over the treasures to be found therein. "Raspberries, Rowena! Mmm, so juicy, and little pastries… I've no idea what's in them, but oh, I've never tasted anything so delicious. They remind me a little of Mrs Hulme's efforts, do you remember, when she was trying to impress Sir Barnaby for Jane, although these are better. Oh, and wine, Rowena. Wine! My goodness, we're being so spoilt, there's nothing like it. I'm so glad you invited me to come with you, dearest. I wouldn't have missed this for the world."

Rowena could not be quite so easy at their circumstances. Her upbringing in a rural rectory had not given her much experience of life beyond her own small parish, but she knew that it was not normal to whisk governesses away for employment of an unknown nature, nor to press heavy purses into her hand and treat her in every respect as if she were a lady. If a distant employer wished to engage a governess, the most she might receive would be the fare for the stage coach.

So she was naturally a little suspicious. Mr Goodenough seemed too jovial a man to be engaged in capturing young women for the slave trade, but there was something havey-cavey about the whole business, and she would not be quite easy until they reached the ducal seat at Staineybank, and she discovered something of the position being offered.

Their neighbour Mr Clark had helpfully provided her with a detailed itinerary of the likely route, which Rowena perused anxiously while Georgie was sampling the contents of the hamper. However, as Woodstock came and went, followed by Enstone and Chapel House, she grew confident that they were, in fact, on the correct road for Brinshire, and began to relax a little.

By the time the first change of horses had been accomplished, and Mr Goodenough had summoned a maid to show them the way to the necessary and had procured hot coffee and fresh rolls to tempt any corner of their appetites left unsatisfied by the hamper, she began to believe this strange journey was really not a hoax at all.

They stopped overnight at Birmingham, where nothing happened to disturb them, and then onwards the next day with another hamper, the mile posts passing in a steady succession. Then they were in Brinshire, passing through the bustling market town of Brinchester and out on the northern side into gentle hills and fertile fields.

An imposing arched gateway appeared, and here they stopped, Mr Goodenough descending to conduct rather a lengthy conversation with the gatekeeper. He needed to produce some papers from an inner pocket, but eventually the gatekeeper was satisfied and the gates creaked open to admit them.

Even Georgie, normally so insouciant, was reduced to awed silence as the house drew into view.

"Oh, Rowena!" she whispered. "So big! You'll get lost in there, I'm certain."

Rowena said nothing, for this was the moment of truth, when she would find out why she was here. Her nerves, somewhat on edge ever since Mr Goodenough's letter had arrived, were now at full stretch. They drew up before the porticoed entrance, and Mr Goodenough hopped down from the box to open the carriage door for them.

As they descended, a footman emerged and skipped down the steps to greet them. Rowena turned to him, ready to give her name, but at one sight of her face, he gasped, turned and ran back into the house.

"Well, that was unexpected," she murmured. "Is my bonnet so askew, Georgie?"

"You look immaculate, as always, dear," Georgie said in puzzled tones.

"Well, no one else is coming out, so shall we go inside?" Rowena said.

Side by side, they mounted the wide steps to the high double doors, which stood wide open, and entered the hall, to find a scene of confusion. Several servants were standing in a huddle, chattering in agitation. One of them, a young housemaid, looked up, saw Rowena approaching, and started to scream.

"No, no, no!" she shrieked, and then ran off, her screams echoing in the distance.

The other servants simply stared at her, mouths hanging open, eyes wide.

"What do you think, Georgie?" Rowena said, unsure whether to scream herself or simply run away. "Have we entered an asylum, do you suppose?"

For answer, Georgie clung to her arm, gripping her so tightly that Rowena was sure she would be bruised.

What on earth sort of place had they arrived at?

4: In The Library

Rowena gazed at the remaining servants, still cowering in a huddle. What was the matter with them? Whatever she had expected to find at Staineybank, this shocked response was frightening. There was no knowing what they might do next.

Fear gave her voice a sharp edge. "This is a fine greeting to a stranger. Who is in charge here?"

An older man stepped forward. "Froggett, ma'am," he whispered.

"And you are... the butler?"

He nodded, shock still written on his face. "Oh, Miss Hester!" he cried, as a woman of middle age emerged from a side room. "Come and see!"

Miss Hester, whoever she might be, looked where he pointed, and she, too, gasped at the sight of Rowena. "Oh, dear God! Where on earth have you come from?"

"From Oxford," Rowena said sharply. "Two days on the road, at the request of someone in this house, and everyone seems astonished to see me. What is the matter with you all?"

"Oh, but—"

The servants scattered suddenly, dropping into low bows as an elderly man of imposing demeanour strode into the hall.

"What is going on?" he began, then he, too, caught sight of Rowena, and his face changed. "What sorcery is this!" he yelled. "How dare you come here, you witch! Get out! Go on, get out of here."

Rowena's patience, already worn to a thread by these unexpected events, gave out completely. "I do not know who you are, sir, for you have not had the courtesy to introduce yourself, but I have seen better manners in a pig farmer. Is this what you call civility in Brinshire? Be assured that I am not here for my own amusement. I was asked to come here, at great inconvenience, and while I do not expect to be treated above my lowly position in society, I draw the line at the sort of arrant rudeness to which I have been exposed today. Certainly, I shall leave. I cannot conceive why you should imagine I wish to stay. Come, Georgie, let us go."

She spun round and marched back to the door and down the steps. There she stopped, aghast. Sitting on the drive all higgledy-piggledy, as if they had simply been thrown from the carriage, were their bags. Of the carriage itself, or Mr Goodenough, there was no sign.

Georgie burst into tears. "Now what are we to do?" she wailed.

"We shall walk back down the drive to the last village we passed," Rowena said stoutly. "It cannot be more than... two or three miles away." Georgie gave a low moan. "There was an inn there where we can bespeak accommodation and send someone for our bags. Then we can— Yes?"

A young man was diffidently trying to attract their attention. "Forgive me, ladies, but pray do not leave. You have given everyone a shock, but if you will forgive us our ill-mannered greeting, you shall see just why we were all so taken aback. I am Richard Merrington, by the way, the duke's heir."

"Miss Rowena Holt, and this is my widowed friend, Mrs Hastings, but we cannot stay, I think. It is clear there is some mischief afoot. I was sent a letter advising me to come here, yet no one seems to be expecting me. Do you have need of a governess here?"

He looked surprised. "Not that I know of."

"A companion, perhaps? I have been seeking employment, you see, and I thought... but it is not so. Someone has played a trick on me."

"And on the duke, I suspect. He is very upset... oh, not with you! Despite his words, he understands that it is not your fault. How can it be?"

"That was the duke over whom I rang a peal, then?"

He grinned, suddenly, looking remarkably boyish. He was a slightly built man of undistinguished appearance but that smile made him appear almost handsome. "It was indeed the duke. I doubt anyone has ever spoken to him in such terms before. That was a moment I will cherish for a long time. But may I not persuade you to come inside, Miss Holt? His grace has asked me to bring you to the library, where you will understand the reason for everyone's dismay, and perhaps you will be so good as to explain further what brought you here. After that, if you still wish to leave, one of his grace's carriages will be at your disposal to take you wherever you wish to go — back to your home, if that is your desire. But please, let your memory of Staineybank not be tarnished by our display of bad manners."

Rowena was not proof against such earnestly expressed courtesy, so she followed him up the steps again to the high ceilinged entrance hall, where he gave instructions for their luggage to be brought into the house.

"Just to keep it safe until you decide whether you will be staying," he said.

He led the way through a succession of sumptuously appointed chambers, and eventually into a room lined floor to ceiling with glass fronted bookcases. The room was large and almost empty, with only three people awaiting them. Rowena recognised the duke, and the woman called Miss Hester was there too. Another man, much of an age with Mr Richard Merrington, was introduced as Mr James Hammond, secretary to his grace.

As Rowena and Georgie were introduced to the duke, he stepped forward and took Rowena's gloved hand. "My dear, forgive an old man for his lack of civility. Staineybank is not normally so deficient in the common courtesies, but you gave us quite a turn. Let me explain to you. Do you see the portrait above the fire? That is the present Duchess of Brinshire, commissioned at the time of her marriage seven years ago. On that wall over there is her predecessor, also painted at the time of her marriage. And on that wall there—"

Rowena gasped. The hair, the clothes, the huge hat were of a style fashionable many years ago, looking outlandish to her eyes. But the face! It was like looking in a mirror, seeing her own features reflected back at her.

"Who is she?" she murmured, her feet carrying her towards the painting of their own volition. "And how? Why? I do not understand!"

"Nor do we," the duke murmured. "She is, or was, the Lady Caroline Bucknell, a daughter of the Duke of Camberley. My first duchess. She is long dead, alas, but you are Caroline to the very life. Her hair had perhaps a shade more curl in it than yours, but perhaps that was only the art of her attendants, who knows? But the colour, and your face… my dear lady, it takes me back so many years. Such a remarkable likeness! You will understand why I thought there must be some dark magic in it."

"Indeed. But I cannot understand why we look so alike. I have no connection to the Duke of Camberley in my family. The Holts have been yeoman farmers in Oxfordshire for centuries, and only latterly hoisted themselves up to more respectable levels. My father was a country rector.

My mother was a Winthrop from Northumberland, but had no living relations. It must be mere coincidence."

"It was not coincidence that brought you here," Mr Merrington said. "You were summoned, you said."

"I had a letter..."

She produced the letter, and Mr Goodenough's card, which were passed around.

"Who is this Goodenough, Hammond?" the duke said.

"I have never heard of him," the secretary said. "I thought I knew every attorney in Brinchester, but not this one... and on Castle Street, too. I must suspect that this man is a fraud."

"Yet someone directed him to bring us here," Rowena said.

"No, to bring *you* here," Mr Merrington said. "It seems reasonable to conclude that someone familiar with the first duchess's portrait has seen you, Miss Holt, and observing the resemblance, has contrived to bring you here, at some expense. Post horses are not cheap, and you had one night on the road, I understand."

"And every comfort provided," Rowena said, "not to mention a purse of one hundred guineas."

Mr Merrington's eyebrows rose. "That is a prodigious sum. Payment of some sort?"

"For incidental expenses, and to allow us to make our own way home if we thought better of the journey."

"So whoever arranged this is a wealthy man," Mr Hammond said, with a little smile. "Benevolent, too, by the sound of it."

"Yes, but *why?*" burst out Rowena. "Why would anyone play such a trick on me... on all of us? It is incomprehensible!"

None of them had an answer.

***

Richard spent that evening at the Assembly Rooms in Brinchester. Never had he regretted the wasted hours more. He had acquitted himself tolerably well on horseback and with a gun, but dancing was not his strongest suit. He could jig about as much as any man, but he suspected that the heir to a dukedom would be expected to produce something more elegant than jigging about.

Besides, he had far rather be at Staineybank finding out more about the intriguing Miss Holt, who had been persuaded to stay at least until Monday while the duke's people endeavoured to discover why she had been summoned there.

Nevertheless, when the duke told him to dance, then dance he must. His sisters, as he had suspected, were thrilled at the possibilities of an assembly in a new place, where they were novelties and not tired faces who had been seen at every assembly for years. Mother dithered about the propriety of dancing so soon after a family bereavement, but given the duke's sanction and the girls' determination to go, she assuaged her conscience by wearing black gloves.

The Brinchester Assembly Rooms were large, brightly lit and already crowded when they arrived.

"So many people," he murmured to Cousin Hester as they made their way from the carriage past the stream of sedan chairs.

She smiled. "The assemblies are very popular. People come in from all the outlying villages and stay at one of the inns overnight. We are fortunate to live close enough to be able to drive home afterwards."

"Are the assemblies popular with the Staineybank household?"

"Very much so. Mr Hammond and Mr Godley come quite often, and the duke accompanies the duchess when she chooses to attend."

"And you?" he said politely.

She laughed. "I come, yes, but not to dance, not any more. The card play is good, however."

"Then I am sorry you will be obliged to forgo the pleasures of the card room, for the far lesser pleasure of watching me try to remember the steps," he said, and she laughed again.

The dancing had begun, but Cousin Hester steered him directly to the Master of Ceremonies, who led him to a girl of no more than seventeen sitting with her mama and watching the dancing avidly.

"Mrs Heale, Miss Heale, may I present to you a gentleman but newly arrived in Brinshire. Mr Merrington is second cousin to His Grace the Duke of Brinshire, and is currently staying with his grace at Staineybank. Sir, may I commend Miss Heale to you as a most desirable partner."

"Miss Heale, would you do me the honour of standing up with me?"

She looked terrified, but her mama's face showed a degree of excitement, with just a hint of calculation. "She would be delighted, wouldn't you, Ann?"

She nodded, Richard offered his hand and they entered the fray. They joined the bottom of a set already in motion at the upper levels, but with some time to wait for the movement to reach them, some conversation was necessary.

"Do you live in Brinchester, Miss Heale?"

"No," she whispered, standing with hands clasped and eyes lowered. Then, feeling that something more might be expected, she added, "High Frickham. We live at High Frickham."

"Is that a pleasant village?"

"Oh, yes." A long pause. "Very pleasant, yes."

Taking pity on her, he said, "I am very new to Brinshire. I have lived my whole life in Norfolk, which is a very flat county, with no hills worth speaking of at all. It is very beautiful, but it is a rather bleak sort of beauty, with a great deal of emptiness. I am looking forward to exploring Brinshire and discovering all its many delights, which will be very different, I am sure. While the weather is fine, I plan to explore the length of the River Brin..."

And so he pattered on, rewarded eventually by a pair of pretty blue eyes raised to his and a tremulous smile. Happily, he was rescued by the dance reaching them, whereupon he discovered that if Miss Heale could not talk, she was a light-footed and graceful dancer, a pleasure to watch. He was able to return her to her mother with a string of compliments that set her blushing, eyes lowered again.

"Lower gentry," Cousin Hester hissed in his ear as he turned away from the Heale's. "A pretty widgeon, but not to be thought of."

"No?" he said, unable to resist teasing her a little. "But she is so pretty."

Cousin Hester raised her eyebrows, an amused look on her face.

The Master of Ceremonies descended again at that point to tow Richard away to another hopeful partner, this one almost bouncing with excitement.

"So you are to be a duke one day," was her opening remark, gazing at him with shining eyes.

"It appears so," he murmured, his heart sinking.

"How wonderful to live at Staineybank. Such a gracious house, I always feel. How lucky you are to live there!"

And from then on, that was the tone of the evening. Word had clearly gone round, and every partner to whom he was introduced eyed him with speculative interest. He could hardly blame them. His appearance at an assembly so soon after the death of the duke's only surviving son would naturally be interpreted as the opening salvo in the campaign to find him a wife. Every mother there was bound to have visions of dear Lucy or Amelia or Clarinda as a duchess, and herself as the heroine of the hour, bringing about the match.

To be truthful, he found it amusing. He had always been a target for such mamas, having a modest estate of his own, but he was now a much bigger prize, possibly the biggest prize on the matrimonial market. There could not be many bachelors at large who would one day wear the coronet of a dukedom. He was even more amused to see that his sisters were receiving their share of attention, too, and his mother was complacently accepting the homage of all the Brinchester matrons as the mother of the next duke.

By the time the supper dance came round, he had had quite enough of adulation and ambition, and would have been relieved to find even one young lady in the throng with whom it was possible to have a conversation that did not circle round, with greater or lesser delicacy, the matter of his inheritance.

Cousin Hester came to his rescue. "This is the time appointed for us to leave, unless you are so enamoured of Brinshire society that you cannot tear yourself away." He raised a sardonic eyebrow, causing her to laugh. "Yes, dire, is it not? But I can confirm that you can dance — not well, but you know the steps, at least, and I feel able to report to his grace that you do not disgrace the Merrington name."

"I thank you for the compliment," he murmured drily.

She laughed again. "I begin to like you, Cousin Richard. Your sisters seem inclined to stay, so make your farewells and let us get out of here."

"You do not wish to retreat to the card room?"

"I do, of course, but I have strict instructions from his grace to bring you home in good time, so that we can be interrogated."

The duke was in the library, hunched over a chessboard with a large candelabrum alongside, engrossed in a game with Miss Holt. Her friend was dozing on a sofa, and Mr Hammond was leafing through a journal.

"You will have to wait, Hester," the duke said without looking up from the board. "I am just about to entrap Miss Holt into checkmate."

Miss Holt merely smiled enigmatically, moved a piece and sat back. Richard sized up the board, chuckled and drew up a chair alongside.

"Are you trying to intimidate me, Mr Merrington?" she said, turning to him with a sweet smile.

"If his grace does not intimidate you, no one will," he said, returning the smile.

"Am I so terrifying, boy?" the duke said.

"You are a duke, sir."

He gave a bark of laughter, and turned his head towards Richard. "You pretend to be as mild as milk, but I think you are not afraid of anyone. You are certainly not afraid of me, are you?"

"Is there any reason why I should be?"

"Ha! You see? And there is another one," he went on, pointing at Miss Holt. "Gave me a piece of her mind this afternoon, and now she has taken one game off me already. Time was when no one would dare to defeat a duke at chess... or any other game, come to that. Treated with proper deference in the old days, we were. But now, you young people think yourselves the equal of anybody."

"Not your equal, your grace," Miss Holt said. "Not in rank, anyway. Now, chess... that is another matter."

"See what I mean?" the duke said. "And the worst of it is, I do not even mind. I look across the board and see my own dear Caroline looking back at me, just as she was when we were first wed, and I will put up with a great deal to have her back again. Hmm... Are you trying to distract me, boy? Let me concentrate on thrashing this impudent woman first."

"I shall look forward to it, sir," he said.

Miss Holt laughed, and when the duke moved his bishop, she shook her head sorrowfully. "Oh, your grace!"

"Now you are trying to bamboozle me into thinking I have made a mistake," the duke said, eyebrows lowered ominously.

"You *have* made a mistake," Richard said, "but it is not irretrievable."

"Mr Merrington!" Miss Holt said. "You are not going to help the duke defeat me, are you? That would be most unchivalrous of you."

"Certainly not, but when *you* have defeated *him*, I should greatly like to test my skills against you. I suspect I should need to be very much on my mettle."

"Think you have the measure of her, do you?" the duke said. "And my position is not irretrievable? Then sit here and you can thrash her for me, if you will."

"Only if the lady permits," he said. "I should not wish to be unchivalrous, after all."

She chuckled. "Very well, but I warn you, I only see one route to victory from your present position."

"I see two," Richard said, taking the seat as the duke vacated it. "Your move, Miss Holt."

"Two! Now I am very much on *my* mettle, sir, but if I move my pawn, so... Ah. I see it now. That was a mistake, was it not? I can see by the look of triumph in your face that it was."

"I hope I should never be so *unchivalrous* as to appear triumphant," he said, swiftly moving his queen.

"Ouch," was all she said. They played swiftly in silence for several turns, before she tipped over her king. "Very good, sir. I confess, I did not see that escape."

"You saw the obvious one, with the knight and bishop, which you blocked with your pawn."

"Yes. Ah, well." The clock on the mantelpiece struck the hour. "What time is it? Good heavens, midnight already. My apologies, your grace, if I have kept you from your bed, and I have certainly kept Mrs Hastings from hers. We shall remedy that situation at once. And thank you — both of you — for some entertaining chess. I bid you a good night."

She dipped a low curtsy, woke her friend and they disappeared.

"An interesting child, however she came to be here," the duke said thoughtfully. "But what of you, boy? Enjoy the assembly, did you?"

"Not a great deal, sir, but I dutifully capered about with a variety of young ladies."

"Capered about, eh?" He chuckled. "How would you describe it, Hester?"

"It is as good a description as any," she said. "He can dance, but not well. He will need lessons before he shows himself at Almack's."

The duke grunted. "Bed, I think. Off you go, boy."

"Yes, sir. Good night, sir."

He bowed, and retreated obediently to his rooms, only taking a wrong turn once.

5: Early Morning

Richard went to bed but not to sleep. His mind was too full to allow him to settle, so he propped himself up with the pillows thinking over all that had happened over the last few days. Less than two weeks since the letter had arrived summoning him to Staineybank, and today only the fifth day since they had left Norwich, yet already so much had happened. He had been tested in riding, gunmanship, estate management and dancing, and next week the search would begin in earnest for a wife for him.

At least he had a brief respite before the onslaught. Tomorrow — no, today, for it was past midnight — was Saturday, and no further tests had been proposed. And then there would be the Sabbath, a day of rest in all civilised households. Two days in which to catch his breath and consider what he was looking for in a wife. What sort of woman would make a good duchess?

It seemed she had to be beautiful, for all three of the portraits of the duke's wives showed very lovely young women. But what else? None of his partners at the assembly had lit any fires in his breast. They were all too shy or too plain or too obviously only interested in his future title. There had not been one with whom he could conduct a rational conversation.

But could they play chess? The thought crept unbidden into his mind, making him smile. Miss Holt was a sterling player, clearly, but Richard had had the incomparable benefit of a tutor of the greatest skill. Joe Ingleton had taught him his letters and numbers, instructed him in the use of the globes, got him speaking French, Latin and a little Greek, instilled in him a lasting love of history and a healthy respect for things that exploded or burnt or poisoned, but he had also shown him how to win at cards without cheating, and how to play chess. Not to win, for Richard had never managed to defeat his tutor, but to analyse the moves and understand how he might have won against a lesser player.

Not that Miss Holt was necessarily a lesser player, for she certainly had some skill, but she had not that ability to analyse the board that Joe had taught him. Few players had it, he suspected, and most of those by instinct, but Joe had given him the key and now he could read a board in a few moments.

He was not sure what to make of Miss Holt. She was lovely, of course, just as lovely as the figure in the portrait, but she was as far from the duchess in rank as it was possible to be, and still be gently born. Her father was nothing but a country rector, from a long line of yeoman farmers, she had said. And she was poor, seeking genteel employment as a governess or paid companion, a fate which had never befallen the Lady Caroline Bucknell. Her clothes were plain, unfashionable and well worn, showing signs of reworking and repair. Her evening gown last night he conceded was a little better, but her hair was simply dressed and she wore no jewellery except a simple cross on a chain around her neck. Beside Lily, the current duchess, even in the deep black of her mourning attire, Miss Holt was a sparrow beside a glossy raven.

Yet she had character, that was undeniable. He smiled in the darkness remembering the robust way she had upbraided the duke on her arrival, and she had not hesitated to challenge him over the chess board. A strong-minded female indeed. Staineybank did not seem quite such an overwhelming place with Miss Holt in it.

He drifted off to sleep, waking only briefly at the sound of a carriage passing by as his mother and sisters returned from the assembly. After that, he slept soundly.

***

Richard woke to birdsong and the gentle rustle of trees touched by a summer breeze. For an instant, the peaceful quietude puzzled him — why was he back at Leahollow? Where was the rumble of traffic and hawkers' cries that prevailed in Norwich? The moment he opened his eyes and saw the ornate carvings on the bedposts and heavy drapery, he remembered with a sigh. Staineybank. His home, now.

It was still early, but he was too restless to lie abed. If he were to spend his days here, then he might as well have it arranged to his satisfaction. He sent for Weston, then went through to the study. It was a good sized square room, with tall windows on one side overlooking the *parterre*, and on the other, windows set high in the wall let in light from an inner courtyard. The furnishings, dark, heavy and very masculine, were arranged as for a sitting room, with a round table and chairs at one side for informal dining, and padded leather chairs set in a circle around the fire. On the walls hung some gloomy paintings of sea battles, dark with smoke, the ships listing on storm-tossed waters.

When Weston arrived, rather bemused to find his master wandering about in his nightgown and showing no interest in dressing, he said, "It seems we shall be permanently fixed here, so I should like a few changes to this room. The table can go, and in its place I should like a desk, like the one I had at Norwich — the one with the lockable top. Also a drawing table, again, just like the one from Winterdale House. If there is nothing suitable here, I shall have that one brought here. And get these paintings down, will you? I never saw anything so depressing. I will send for some from Winterdale, or possibly from Leahollow. There is more wall to be filled here than at Winterdale. Oh, and a bookcase of some sort. This room was used by former heirs to the dukedom, but they do not seem to have been fond of reading. Or perhaps they found all the books they needed in the library, but I like my own books near at hand. I shall work in here whenever the duke has nothing else for me to do."

"Yes, sir," Weston said. "I will see what I can do."

"Good. Froggett will know what furniture they have stuffed away in the attics. Are there attics? I assume there are."

"There are, sir. My own quarters are there."

"Excellent. Have you brought my water, Weston? I shall dress now, I think."

Richard arrived at the breakfast parlour in good spirits, having managed to find his way there quite unaided for the first time. Staineybank was a house of vast size, but it had a degree of symmetry that made its succession of apartments less mystifying than in some houses, and since every room connected with the next, if one were entirely lost one need only walk from room to room around the perimeter until one arrived where one wanted to be.

Being so early, he had expected to be the first there, but Mr Hammond was already tucking into a mutton chop, and Miss Holt and Mrs Hastings were also there, neatly but plainly dressed, as yesterday. Perhaps they had no other style of garments, or merely preferred simplicity.

After bowing to the ladies, and determining that they had everything they needed, Richard sat as Froggett poured coffee for him, laid two slices of ham on his plate and placed the basket of toast within reach. His third breakfast at Staineybank and already the servants had learnt his habitual meal.

"Did you enjoy a comfortable night, Miss Holt?" he said, since she was sitting directly opposite him, watching him with clear grey eyes.

"I would have to be excessively hard to please if I had not," she said, a little smile playing on her lips. "I have never been so commodiously accommodated in my life before. I am disappointed to find that there is no need for either a governess or companion at Staineybank, for I should be happy to spend the rest of my life in such luxury, I assure you. I shall be very sorry to leave."

"You will not leave too precipitately, I trust?" he said politely. "Not before I have had an opportunity to test myself fully against your skills at chess."

"We cannot leave before Monday unless we wish to spend the Sabbath at a posting house, so I believe you may have your opportunity, Mr Merrington. But pray tell me, for my friend and I were trying to puzzle it out, why is it that the heir to the dukedom has no title? For that is the custom, is it not — a marquessate or an earldom, or something of the sort?"

"That is so for an heir in the direct line — a son or grandson. But I am merely a second cousin once removed, so I am plain Mr Merrington."

"Ah, that makes sense. You were right, Georgie."

Mrs Hastings smiled. "That's what comes of living across the road from Mr Childs, who must read his copy of the Peerage before bed instead of the Bible, he knows it so well. The poor little boy who died was a marquess, remember?"

"The Marquess of Losseter," Mr Hammond said, his face clouding. "The fourth son of the present duke to bear the title, and the fourth to be buried. Her grace feels it exceedingly, but his grace is resigned to his losses. That is why he has now sent for Mr Merrington."

"Then you did not grow up here?" Miss Holt said in astonished tones.

Richard shook his head. "I only arrived two days before you did."

"But you must have visited... as a boy, surely? As a cousin..."

Another shake of the head. "I never met his grace until this week. My father met him once, quite by chance, in town. On being introduced, the duke said, *'Good day to you, Merrington'*, and that was the end of it. Apart from that, the only contact we ever had was a letter now and then announcing the birth of a son, knocking us back in the succession, or a death, which raised us up. And when I moved to Norwich from my estate at Leahollow, I wrote to let him know my new direction. That is all the contact between the two branches of the family, until now. So I am just as new to Staineybank as you are Miss Holt, and if you want to find the Green Drawing Room or the Bishop's Chamber or the Florence Room, it is of no use to apply to me."

"Are there such rooms?"

"Apparently so. The duke mentioned them at dinner one night."

With a hint of amusement in his voice, Mr Hammond said, "There is a framed plan of the house on the wall of the library."

"Thank you. I shall study it carefully, for I am sure to be tested on such matters before too long," Richard said, making Miss Holt laugh.

For a while, they all ate in silence. Mr Hammond, having tucked away a quantity of food that Richard could not even contemplate so early in the day, rose, bowed to the ladies and then to Richard, and disappeared about his secretarial duties.

Miss Holt had stopped eating some time ago, but she had refilled her coffee cup several times. Now she set the cup down and said, "May I enquire, Mr Merrington, and tell me to mind my own business if I am too intrusive, but why did you move to Norwich? You had an estate, I think you said?"

"Still have it, in fact, but it is leased out. It is a question of money, Miss Holt. My income is not large, and I have my mother and four sisters to support. It seemed better to me to live economically in town and rent out Leahollow, thus reducing my expenditure and increasing my income in one judicious move."

"Do you prefer, then, to live in the town rather than the country?"

"There are advantages to both, I feel. Town has the convenience of many facilities and a greater society, but the country has the clean air and open spaces that nourish the soul — or my soul, at any rate. What of you, Miss Holt? Do you prefer the town or country?"

"I am perfectly happy to live anywhere where someone will employ me," she said, her eyes twinkling merrily. "Beggars cannot be choosers, as the saying is, Mr Merrington."

He frowned, setting down his own coffee cup. "You are determined, then, to seek a post? Have you no alternative? The life of a governess is a hard one, and even a companion is not always treated as a member of the family."

"I am aware of it, sir, but I am in no position to be too particular. When my father died, he left me almost penniless. His brother, my uncle, took me in, but when he died..." She paused, some expression crossing her face that he could not identify. "Well, I had to move on. My friend took me in temporarily, but I cannot exhaust her kindness, so I must earn my keep. If I cannot find a position as a governess, then it will have to be a school."

"Why not a husband?" he burst out, before he could stop himself. "Forgive my impertinence, Miss Holt, but with your looks, I find it hard to understand why you have not an army of suitors vying for your hand. With a husband, you would be able to retain your proper sphere in society, and not be at the beck and call of a gaggle of unruly children."

She blushed rather charmingly, but merely shook her head.

It was Mrs Hastings who answered. "In my experience, husbands are not the reliable ticket to a lifetime of prosperity they are purported to be."

Miss Holt laughed. "You were singularly unfortunate in Henry dying so young, my dear, but at least you had a dowry which provides you with an annuity. I never had a penny to my name."

"That is not an insuperable problem," Richard murmured. "A wealthy man would not care."

"Oh, a *wealthy* man, true," Miss Holt said, smiling. "And they are as common as daisies around country rectories, naturally. I was turning down three a day, and four on Sundays."

Richard did not feel he could pry further, but to him it was astonishing that so lovely a girl was still unwed at... it was hard to tell, but she must be above one and twenty. She had pleasant manners and an agreeable disposition, and no faults that he could discern. She had every admirable quality for a wife, and yet no one had snapped her up. Or perhaps she had chosen not to be snapped up, who could tell?

After breakfast, he made his way back to his apartments, to find his study crawling with footmen carrying furniture about and maids cleaning the new items, and all of them getting in each other's way. In a chair by the fireplace, the duke sat in a voluminous banyan and nightcap, a cup of chocolate in his hand.

"Good morning, your grace. I hope all this commotion did not disturb you."

"Not at all. Pleased to see you are getting settled in, boy," he said genially. "I had forgotten that desk — my mother used to use it. But what is that thing for, by the window?"

"It is a drawing table, sir. The top tilts to make it easier to draw on. I am amazed that you have such a thing here."

"So am I. Never seen it before, to be honest. Froggett, why do we have a contraption like that?"

"The architect left it behind, your grace, after working on the designs for the Dower House."

"Which never got built, since my mother died before a stone could be laid. You draw a bit, then, boy?"

"I do, sir."

"Got anything we can see?"

Richard hesitated, but there was no avoiding the moment when everyone would know about his hobby. His profitable hobby, if the truth were told. So went through to his bedroom, and returned with a book.

"This is what I draw, sir."

The duke set down his chocolate, and opened the book at the title page. "*'A Collection of Designs for Cottages, Both Modern and Healthy,*

Suitable for the Accommodation of Labourers and their Families, With Complete Estimates of Materials'. What nonsense is this?"

"Exactly what it says, sir. Designs for cottages. I had occasion to build some new cottages at Leahollow, so I designed them myself and worked out how much wood, how many bricks, how many pounds of nails, and so forth. I then repeated the work for various different designs and had them printed. That way, the plans can be handed over to a local builder, who need only follow the simple instructions. And it can easily be costed out." He paused, seeing the duke's eyebrows as low as they had ever been. "The book has been very popular. It is in its third edition, and I have been asked to produce a second collection, with gatehouses, barns and stables included."

"*'By a Gentleman'*. So you are too ashamed to put your name to it?"

"I did not want to involve the Merrington name, or do anything that might reflect badly on you, your grace."

"Poppycock! You are ashamed of it. Labourers' cottages, indeed! Why on earth do you do it?"

"I enjoy it," Richard said in surprise. "It brings in a little extra money, too, but mostly I find the work satisfying, and useful, too. There are plenty of estates where the landlord wishes to rebuild his cottages, but not run up excessive expense with architect's fees. Nor does he necessarily trust a local builder to do the job from the ground up, letting the costs mount up. This book is perfect for such a case."

"Pft! What a ridiculous idea! Well, you will stop all this nonsense, right now. I will not have my heir involved in anything so sordid as publishing books. If it were poetry, perhaps, or some learned tome, I might overlook it, but this is unacceptable. It will have to stop, do you hear me, boy?"

Richard took a deep breath. "I hear you, your grace, but I have no intention of giving up a hobby that gives me pleasure and is harmless."

The duke growled deep in his throat. "Do you defy me, boy?"

"In this matter, I am afraid I must, your grace."

"Did I not tell you to address me as *'Duke'*? Why do you persist in calling me *'your grace'* like a servant?"

"I shall stop calling you *'your grace'* when you stop calling me *'boy'*, sir."

The duke stared at him for a long moment, but Richard refused to drop his own gaze.

Abruptly the duke chuckled. "You have some spirit, Richard. I like that."

"Thank you, Duke."

The servants, who had frozen in place, holding their breath, began to move about again.

The duke drained his chocolate and rose to his feet. "My study, one hour from now."

"Yes, sir."

Richard bowed as the duke strode through the door. Then he crossed the room to where the drawing desk was being manoeuvred into position by two burly footmen, and gently ran his hands over the surface. Yes, it would do.

He smiled.

6: Visitors

The duke's study was a small room off the library, and should more properly have been described as Mr Hammond's study, for his was the only desk therein. Saturday, it seemed, was the duke's day for dealing with correspondence, so two hours were spent in Mr Hammond reading out each letter, after which the duke would give his instruction. "Burn it," seemed to be a common response, but occasionally he would issue orders for the bailiff or gamekeeper or head groom or some other factotum, and sometimes he would formulate a reply for Mr Hammond to write.

Richard was sure that the duke intended his presence as a punishment for daring to flout his wishes, but in truth he found it fascinating. Not so much for the letters themselves, for they dealt with people and places and situations quite unknown to him, but for the insight it gave him into the duke's mind. He never hesitated over his response, and never asked for advice. It was an object lesson in decisive management.

Yet the scale of his operations was immense. Even at Staineybank, there were farms, mills, whole villages in one or two cases, entirely owned by the duke, and much more elsewhere in England. Richard was no stranger to estate management, but this was on a scale he had never imagined. And one day the responsibility for all of it would be his. It was both humbling and terrifying.

When the duke had disappeared for his daily tour of the stables, Richard lingered on in Mr Hammond's study, examining the maps pinned to the wall showing the duke's properties while the secretary's pen scratched away, replying to those few letters that the duke had deemed worthy of a response.

Eventually, he laid down his pen. "Do you have any questions, Mr Merrington?"

Richard gave a wry laugh. "It is too overwhelming for questions, Mr Hammond."

"Has his grace talked to you about money yet?"

"No, not a word. I should be interested to see the accounts, but there is time enough for that, I dare say. Have you worked here for long?"

"Unofficially, since I was a boy. My father was secretary before me, so I helped out and when he retired two years ago, I took over and now he helps me out sometimes. We are working together on his grace's memoirs, compiled from his diaries. Fascinating stuff, as you can imagine. He has had a very colourful life."

"Has he?"

Mr Hammond laughed. "Did you not follow him in the newspapers? His speeches in the House, his appearances at court, his travels in France, before the upstart Corsican made it difficult?"

"We took the Norwich Mercury, but he was not mentioned a great deal in that."

That brought another spurt of laughter. "How lowering to know that his own cousin took no interest in his grace's movements."

"Second cousin, once removed," Richard said, smiling. "My father always felt that, since his grace chose to pretend we did not exist, we should extend the same courtesy to him. I have never had any quarrel with that point of view. But tell me, what do you make of Miss Holt? Is there any obvious connection to the Lady Caroline Bucknell?"

"None that I could find. I talked to her for some time after you went off to caper about in Brinchester, and there is certainly no likely connection on the Holt side. Her mother... nothing is known of her, so there might be something there, but the most likely connection is... um, irregular."

"That is my thought also," Richard said. "If the connection were legitimate, it would be well known."

"Exactly. Miss Holt seemed to accept the possibility with equanimity."

Richard smiled. "She is a redoubtable lady."

Cousin Hester put her head round the door, a puzzled expression on her face which lightened when she saw Richard. "There you are, sir. I have been searching for you all over the house. I have had some good fortune with the wife-hunting. The Earl and Countess of Yeldon will be here tonight with their three daughters, all unmarried and extremely eligible. Lord Yeldon will put up thirty thousand for whichever of them you marry. Is that not excellent news? We could have you settled in no time."

Beaming, she bustled away, leaving Richard despondent.

Mr Hammond chuckled. "Your face is a picture, Mr Merrington. I take it you were not expecting to be accosted quite so soon? And the worst of it is, they live just far enough away that they will be obliged to stay the night, and tomorrow being the Sabbath..."

Richard groaned. "I was looking forward to a couple of peaceful days, at least, and now I shall have three — *three!* — eligible young ladies hanging on my sleeve. What are they like, Mr Hammond?"

But he only laughed, and said, "You will see, Mr Merrington. You will see."

There was still work going on in his study, so Richard found an old coat and, after only a little blundering about, found the way out to the terrace, and thence to the *parterre.* After walking about for some time, he wearied of the formality and set off on a path that led past formal flower beds before meandering promisingly towards a shrubbery.

Before he left the formal gardens behind, however, he came upon an elegant little herb garden with a fountain in the centre. Sitting on a carved wooden bench staring at the water was Miss Holt.

With a smile and a bow, Richard called out, "Good day to you, Miss Holt!"

"Oh!" She looked up, startled from her reverie. "It is you, Mr Merrington. What a fine, sunny day, is it not? Just the day to enjoy these splendid gardens."

"Are they splendid? I find them rather old-fashioned, myself. I prefer a more pastoral setting. But I intrude upon your solitude. Forgive me."

"No intrusion, sir. I am always glad of company, and if you understand how this device works, I should be glad to hear an explanation."

He walked forward and sat on the other end of the bench. "Device? Do you mean the fountain?"

"Precisely. I have never seen one before, you see, so I have no idea how the water keeps spouting. Is there a stream underground which drives it?"

"Possibly. That is one way, but the usual way is to have a supply of water at a higher level than the fountain. My father had one built at

Leahollow, and it was supplied by a small reservoir on a hill. One could open a sluice gate and water would descend from the reservoir through pipes to the fountain, where the force of the water would drive it up into the air. Ours was a little larger than this, but just as effective."

"It is so soothing, I find. The sound of the water quite lulls me into tranquillity. How lucky you are to live in this wonderful place, Mr Merrington."

"Perhaps."

She turned to face him fully, so that her lovely face was only a few feet away from him, and his breath caught at the sight. So beautiful! Yet no man had succeeded in tempting her into matrimony. For she must have had admirers, that was beyond dispute.

"You sound uncertain, sir. Do you not like Staineybank?"

"It matters not one whit whether I like it or not. It is my home now and forever."

"Ah. Yes, it would be natural to resent it... the upheaval, for you and your mother and sisters, too. You were settled at Norwich, and now you must leave it all behind, brought here by the duke's command, a hostage to fortune."

"We are both hostages to fortune, it seems to me," he said slowly. "I by the chance death of a boy of six years, and you by the deaths of your father and then your uncle."

"Not quite," she said. "You see, I had a choice. When my uncle died, my cousin inherited and brought his wife and children to live at Greenwood House. They inherited me, as well, and at first that worked well, because I offered to teach the children and saved them the cost of a governess. But Maria, my cousin's wife, never liked me. Superficially she treated me well, as a member of the family, just like her own sister who also lived with us, but… oh, the mistress of the house has a thousand ways to chip away at one. Little criticisms of schoolroom lessons, for instance, or a hint that I put myself forward when visitors called, or had done something to upset her sister. My cousin saw none of it, and thought we were in perfect harmony, but I could not go on letting her gradually grind me into dust. I persuaded her to give me a reference as a governess, and went to Mrs Hastings. But I confess, it has not been as easy to find a position as I had hoped."

"Then stay here a little longer," Richard said. "Write your applications on Staineybank paper, and franked by the duke. That might open a few doors."

She chuckled. "Oh yes, but I could not possibly impose on his grace in that way. There is a school in Oxford which will take me, I am sure. I know one of the teachers there, and she will put in a word for me. I shall not starve, I assure you."

"I am sure you will not, but being a governess or a schoolmistress is likely to be just as dispiriting as life with your cousin's wife. I should not like you to be ground into dust, Miss Holt."

She smiled at him, so that again he was momentarily breathless. "You are very good, sir, but I have no intention of being ground into dust. Ah, here is Mrs Hastings now. Have you finished your letters, my dear? Then let us explore a little more of these wonderful gardens. Thank you for your company, Mr Merrington. We shall see you at dinner, no doubt."

She sailed off arm in arm with her friend without a backward glance, but Richard found himself despondent again. Dinner would bring with it the Earl and Countess of Yeldon and their three eligible daughters, and two days of matchmaking. It was not an enticing prospect.

***

Rowena had already worn her best evening gown the previous night, but with even more titled personages descending on Staineybank, there was no help for it but to wear it again. Georgie was even more stretched, for she had nothing so fine. However, they arranged each other's hair in more elaborate styles, and with some careful use of ribbon, and a shawl apiece, they sallied downstairs to the White Drawing Room.

The first thing they saw was Mr Merrington sitting in a gaggle of unknown ladies. Miss Hester Merrington bustled forward to introduce them first to the Earl and Countess of Yeldon, who were sitting with the duchess and her sister. They made the slightest inclination of their heads towards Rowena and Georgie, then turned away, uninterested. After that, they curtsied to the Yeldons' son and heir, Viscount Harper, who raised a quizzing glass before making them a perfunctory bow. Finally they were introduced to the three Harper ladies, indistinguishable with their pale gowns, blonde hair and big blue eyes, who giggled and whispered to each other behind their fans. Rowena and Georgie made their curtsies and moved swiftly away, for the Harper family was not there to see two impoverished and temporary guests. The daughters had already latched onto their quarry, poor Mr Merrington, who bore rather a hounded look.

The Merrington ladies had spotted quarry of their own in the young Viscount Harper, who was soon holding court to all four of them. He looked bored, and since they were all older than he was and making no secret of their interest, it was not to be wondered at.

Rowena and Georgie found a quiet corner, and settled down to be as unobtrusive as possible. Mr Godley took pity on them and perched on the edge of a chair beside Rowena, leaning eagerly towards her as he spoke. Her gown was not cut low at the front, but he was so tall that his eyes wandered downwards anyway. She was relieved when Froggett announced dinner, and even more relieved when Mr Godley jumped forward to escort one of the earl's daughters.

Many more ladies than gentlemen gathered around the dining table, so Rowena had no expectation of finding a gentleman beside her, but to her surprise she was seated between Mr Hammond, his grace's secretary, and Viscount Harper. The former she already knew to be a pleasant man and an easy conversationalist, but she was agreeably surprised to find that the viscount, despite his young age, was both attentive and amusing, trying very gently to flirt with her. She supposed that he regarded her as a safe object for his gallantry, since she could have no possible expectation of securing him as a husband. She could not fault him for trying his wings a little, or for avoiding the risk of entangling himself with one of the hopeful Merrington ladies.

Across the table and near enough for her to hear all that was said, she could see Mr Merrington and one of the Harper ladies — Lady Diana, she thought, the middle one. She was a boisterous sort of girl, practically bouncing in her chair as she spoke, hands waving in the air to emphasise each point. Mr Merrington looked bemused, as well he might.

On his other side he had the eldest of the sisters, Lady Agatha, who was very much the opposite. To every opening on his part, she seemed to reply more or less at random. When he asked about her home, she explained that she was engaged on stitching roses for a cushion for the summer parlour in five different colours — white, pale pink, a deeper pink, red and yellow. "I like the yellow best," she confided. "Although the pale pink is very pretty, too. And the white... yes, I do think I like the white best. When I have finished the flowers, I shall start on the stems. That will be green... or brown... no, I think I prefer green." When he asked if the estate had extensive grounds, she told him about her horse, improbably called

Janet, which had four white socks and a white flash on her forehead. Mr Merrington looked as if he were struggling to stay awake.

When the ladies withdrew, the earl's daughters lounged about the drawing room, yawning and stretching and making disparaging remarks in low voices about the old fashioned decorations and furnishings in the room. When the duchess came across to them, however, they complimented her in glowing terms on the magnificence of the apartments at Staineybank.

"Oh, magnificent, yes," the duchess said, "but not a comfortable place to live, in my view."

"Oh, no, no!" they chorused. "Such splendour! Such opulence! And the paintings so inspiring!"

Rowena looked around at the array of portraits of elderly men in their robes of state or the bewigged grandeur of judges, and wondered what there was to inspire anyone, let alone a young lady. She had never had anything to do with the aristocracy before, but she was not gaining a good impression of it from the display at Staineybank. Even the duke, despite his softening since their initial contretemps, was nothing if not autocratic, especially to his heir. Poor Mr Merrington! He might look forward to a life of unimaginable wealth and ease, but he would pay a high price for it if he had to marry someone like the Harper sisters.

As soon as the gentlemen began to reappear, the earl's daughters rushed to the instrument.

"Oh do let us open the pianoforte, dear Duchess! We long for a little music, do we not, Mama?"

"Oh yes," their mother said, her eyes fixed on the door to watch who was arriving. "Do let us have some music."

Thus it was that when Mr Merrington and the duke entered the room, one of the sisters — was it Lady Frederica? — was playing a lively Italian air, while the other two sang a duet. It was not that they were poor performers, for they had clearly been well taught and had practised diligently, but they would have done better to attend to the performance rather than casting their eyes around the room to see how it was received. All three took a turn to play, before the duchess said very firmly that she was sure one or two of the Merrington sisters would like to perform next.

It was not one or two, but all four of them, and it was clear that they had practised less diligently. Still, music meant no conversation, and since Mr Godney was now hovering nearby again, Rowena was glad of the reprieve. She was rather hopeful that would see the end of the music, for the tea tray had been and gone, after which she could retire to bed and escape these dreadful people. But there was one uncomfortable interlude still awaiting her.

When the last sister had risen from the instrument, and the duke was beginning to call for the card tables, Mr Merrington said, "There are still some young ladies who have not yet had an opportunity to delight us. Miss Willaston?" But the duchess's sister shook her head, blushing violently. "Miss Holt, then. I am sure you play, ma'am."

"I do but I believe his grace is ready for a change of activity, and I would not wish to keep him from the card table."

But the duke surprised her. "You play, do you? Then come, take your place, young lady, and let us hear what you can do."

There was no help for it. Rowena knew that her abilities would pass muster anywhere, but she also knew that tact required the governess not to outshine the daughters of the upper ranks. As she took her place on the stool, its cushion warmed by the several previous occupants, she thought furiously. In the end, she settled on a simple Scotch air to which she knew the words.

It seemed that others knew the words, too, for first the duke joined in and then several others, and the audience liked it so well that she was adjured to play another. She demurred, however, for she could see that several of the company were hiding their yawns.

As she rose to leave the instrument, the duke bowed to her and lifted her hand to his lips. "My dear, that was delightful. I cannot thank you enough for bringing my dear Caroline back to life, not only in appearance but in voice as well. I shall look forward to many more such pleasures from you, but for now let us entertain our guests with a little card play. You will partner me at whist, I trust? For the duchess does not play with enthusiasm, but I am sure that *you* do."

She could not deny it, and so for the second night running, the duke kept her out of her bed many hours after she had been longing to escape. She did not mind humouring him a little, but she felt so out of place at Staineybank amongst the haughty aristocracy that she could not wait to leave it. Monday! On Monday she could finally escape, and the only person she would spare a thought for after she departed would be poor Mr Merrington.

7: A Marriage Is Proposed

Richard was not sure how he survived Sunday. The earl's daughters were lurking at the bottom of the stairs as soon as he went down, and they clung to him, sometimes literally, for the entire day. They seemed to take it in turns to be the one monopolising his attention, while the other two loitered nearby awaiting their turn. Apart from Lady Agatha the banal, and Lady Diana the boisterous, he discovered that Lady Frederica was the amorous type, who whispered hints into his ear of what she would very much like him to do to her and even attempted to kiss him behind a yew tree in the garden.

Even in the chapel, they sat in a row behind him, whispering and giggling together, until even his mother, normally the most tolerant of the ways of the nobility, felt obliged to turn round with a finger to her lips. Not that it did a bit of good. They seemed impervious to hints.

In the evening, when the ladies had withdrawn and Richard was looking forward to a blessedly peaceful hour with the gentlemen and the port, the duke wiggled his eyebrows, and said, "Well now, Richard, what do you think?"

"Think, sir? About what?"

"About the young ladies, Yeldon's girls. Pretty little things, are they not? Which one did you like best?"

"There is thirty thousand for whichever one you choose," Lord Yeldon said.

They turned to him expectantly. For an instant, Richard panicked. He had to choose one of them that very minute — choose a wife from the three dire prospects on offer, any one of whom would drive him to Bedlam within a month. Yet how could he possibly escape his fate? His neckcloth felt unexpectedly tight, like a noose around his neck.

It was Lord Harper who saved him and gave him time to think. "M'sisters are all silly widgeons, would you not agree, Merrington? Not a sensible thought in their feather heads."

The duke gave a rumble of laughter. "A man always thinks his sisters are widgeons. Different matter when a fellow is looking for a wife, though. He sees beneath the surface, eh, Richard? Any of them take your fancy?"

"The Lady Agatha, the Lady Diana and the Lady Frederica have many estimable qualities," he said, thinking quickly. "They are beautiful, accomplished and elegant, and undoubtedly will make excellent marriages in due course. If I were as settled in my position in society as you gentlemen are, I should certainly choose just such a wife, and she would be able to play and sing all day long, and lighten the spirits of everyone in the household. She need do nothing else but flutter through life like a butterfly. Unfortunately, in my present situation, I need a wife who is less refined and more robust...

someone who is more in keeping with my less exalted upbringing, who understands the chasm that I must jump if I am to be duke one day. I need a wife who understands the realm of the lower gentry, which the daughters of an earl can never do."

The duke's brows lowered a little, but the earl nodded sagely. "Ah, yes, my girls are pearls above price."

As they left the dining room to return to the ladies, Mr Hammond said in a low voice to Richard, "Neatly done, sir. An elegant escape."

Richard only smiled.

***

Rowena was up early on Monday morning, kneeling beside her small box, folding and packing.

Georgie, still only half awake, murmured, "We're not leaving immediately, are we? A decent breakfast is necessary to fortify us for the journey."

"Oh yes, but I want to be ready. I cannot wait to leave this place."

"Really? Waited on hand and foot, a bath every day if we want it, and the table groaning with food twice a day, and a hot supper, too. I agree the company isn't wonderful, but I could put up with it a little longer... indefinitely, in fact, if it were offered."

Rowena sat back on her heels, smiling. "Indeed, I enjoy all that, too, and the company has been fascinating if not the most agreeable in the world. I have never bumped shoulders with the nobility before. The nearest was old Sir Harold, remember him? Such a dear! But baronets do not count, whereas here there is a duke, an earl and countess, and a viscount, not to mention three actual ladies. Do you not find them intriguing? So different from mere mortals like us. They float through life doing exactly as they please, and everyone bows down to them and makes their lives easy. Not one of them has ever had to earn a living, as I must do. And the sooner the better, my dear friend, for I cannot rely on your good nature any longer."

When the maid came with their hot water, Rowena said, "Would you be so good as to ask if we might have the use of a carriage after breakfast to take us to the nearest post house? We will take up a post chaise from there."

The girl was soon back, her face a little pink. "Mr Froggett sends 'is compliments, miss, an' sorry to be disobligin', but 'is grace 'as given orders that if you was to ask for a carriage, to speak to 'is grace first. An' please not to go down for breakfast today, cos his lordship an' fam'ly is leavin'. Cook'll send trays up for you."

"So, no early start for us, then," Rowena said fretfully. "Well, no matter. We can still be home by tomorrow, God willing."

"It sounds as if his grace doesn't want you to leave at all," Georgie said, rolling over and pushing herself upright on the edge of the bed, adding gloomily, "but I'm sure you'll persuade him. I'd better start packing, too."

"Or perhaps he wants to offer his carriage for the whole journey, complete with footmen and outriders," Rowena said, with a gurgle of merriment. "That would be something, would it not?"

"Ooh, yes! Can you imagine Mr Clark's face?"

"Or Mrs Burnley! It would be the talk of the parish for months. But it is hardly likely, so I shall use a little of my hundred pounds on a post chaise and four. That will be stylish enough for me."

"Four horses! How extravagant!" Georgie said.

After that, the two settled to their packing.

With the breakfast trays brought and finished with, the packing completed and the two dressed in their travelling gowns and pelisses, ready for departure, they found a vantage point above the entrance and watched the earl and his family depart in a train of three carriages, accompanied by footmen, outriders and a little army of valets and lady's maids. Only then did Rowena feel it safe to descend and enquire for the duke.

"In the library, madam," the butler said. "This way."

"We know the way," Georgie mouthed at Rowena, who smiled and shrugged.

Reaching the library, a footman beside the door threw it open and the butler stepped through it in front of Rowena and Georgie.

"Mrs Hastings and Miss Holt, your grace," he intoned, then bowed low.

The duke, his face thunderous, was standing facing Mr Merrington, who bore his usual genial expression. Nearby, Mr Hammond looked anxious. It seemed that they had disturbed a quarrel of some sort, but the duke turned to them at once, his face abruptly wreathed in smiles.

"Ah, my dear ladies!" the duke said, then, seeing their travelling clothes, went on, "But you are not leaving us, surely?"

"I am afraid that we must, your grace," Rowena said. "You and her grace have been all that is kind and generous towards us, but we were drawn here on false pretences and must not trespass on your hospitality any longer."

"But you have hardly been here any time, and it has been such a pleasure. I had hoped you would stay longer, to humour an old man. Surely I can persuade you?"

"You are too good," Rowena said with feeling, "but I have a living to earn, and have no claim on you. You have no need for a governess, unfortunately, nor for a companion, so I must seek employment elsewhere."

"Your similarity to my first duchess surely gives you some family connection, but if you think that is too tenuous, then let the claim of friendship sway you."

She shook her head. "I cannot take advantage of you any longer, your grace. I could only agree to stay if I have employment here, and I do not see any opening for me. What could I do that would be of use to you? How might I serve you? What could I be?"

Mr Merrington stepped forward with a deprecating little cough. "You could be my wife. You could marry me."

The duke grunted, and even Mr Hammond made a small *'Huh!'* of surprise.

Rowena laughed. There was no other possible reaction. It was a joke, surely? Rather a cruel one, perhaps, but no less a joke for all that. "You are not serious, sir."

"Indeed I am, Miss Holt. I was never more serious in my life. I beg your pardon for taking you by surprise, but if you give me a little time, I am sure I can come up with more fitting words for a proposal."

Georgie tugged at Rowena's sleeve. "This is the point where you thank the gentleman politely and accept his most obliging offer."

Mr Merrington laughed at that. "I do not expect you to answer me at once, Miss Holt. You will wish to think about it."

Puzzled, Rowena turned to the duke. "Your grace, you surely cannot approve of such a match — the daughter of a clergyman to marry a future duke? It is impossible!"

The duke shrugged. "Richard has made it very clear that he will choose his own wife, and he seems not to like the starchy high-ranking ladies he has met so far. Cannot say I liked them much myself. My Caroline was from the highest ranks but she was never stuffy, like Yeldon's girls. Now Jane, my second duchess... well, the less said about her the better. But Lily's father is nobody at all, minor gentry, and I have been very happy with her. She is too timid, perhaps, but you are not timid, I think, Miss Holt. You will do well enough for Richard, if that is what he wants, and you will both have time to grow accustomed to the future that awaits you, since I have no plans to be carted off to the mausoleum just yet. So take him, if you want. I shall not cut up rough."

Rowena felt the ground sliding from beneath her feet. What was she to do? She could only stare at the duke, and then at Mr Merrington. What on earth was she to do?

***

Richard poured two glasses of wine, and placed one on the table beside Miss Holt's chair. Mr Hammond had persuaded them both into the study *'to have a private chat'*, as he put it. Miss Holt had doffed her bonnet and gloves, but she still wore her faded travelling pelisse. Oddly, his immediate thought was that at least she would have new clothes now, new and finer clothes. He had a longing to see her in silk and jewels.

He took a sip of his wine, then took the chair opposite hers. "I must again beg your pardon for—"

"Why?" she burst out. "Why on earth would you marry someone like me?"

He sipped again, musing. "I could probably give you any number of logical reasons... or practical ones, anyway. But this is not a matter of logic. I had not thought of it at all, indeed whatever ideas were in my head were along the lines of what I did *not* want in a wife. I have been provided with much material in that way these last two days." She smiled at that, understanding him perfectly. "But when you said you were leaving, I knew very clearly and unequivocally that I did not want you to leave. Thus my proposal."

"But that is—"

"Crazy? Impulsive? Reckless? Yes, all of those. To decide on a wife almost on a whim — it does seem like madness. But now that it is done, I am entirely at ease with my decision. You are absolutely the right wife for me, of that I am certain, but if you asked me to explain my reasons, I am not sure I could do it. It is too irrational. I am sorry for the abruptness of it, but I could not let the moment pass by. You asked how you could possibly stay, and I am offering you a way. If you want it. But you do not have to decide at once. Take as much time as you need to consider."

He watched as she rose and walked to the window, gazing out at the gardens. The study was directly below his dressing room, so he knew she would have a view over the *parterre*, although perhaps she would not even notice the view. She would be mulling over in her mind the prospect of Richard as a husband. He was not imposing, as the duke had pointed out. He was no more than average height, not well-built or athletic, not especially handsome, clothed still for his position as a gentleman of limited means.

But would she put up with his undistinguished self for the life of ease that he could offer her? Her home would be Staineybank, she would be waited on by a veritable army of servants, and when she went to London, she would cause a stir in any room she entered because she would be a duchess. She would never need to be the downtrodden governess to a horde of undisciplined children, criticised by their mama and possibly preyed on by their papa, living in constant fear of a dismissal that would render her destitute. She could not refuse him... could she?

As she turned away from the window, he saw her face was sad. Was this to be a rejection? Would she tell her pupils in years to come that she had once turned down the chance to be a duchess? Would it comfort her old age that she could have been wealthy if only the man had been better looking or taller or had broader shoulders?

"You say nothing of love," she said.

That was unexpected! "It would be hypocritical of me to speak of affection when we have only known each other for... what is it? Barely three days. What do we know of each other? You like duck and asparagus, you play and sing beautifully, you are a skilful chess player. I dare say you know even less of me. But even if we cannot claim to be in love, there is an affinity between us... at least on my side. I feel at ease with you, as I have not felt with anyone else at Staineybank. You are everything that is admirable in a woman. You stood up to the duke when he was rude to you that first day, which was splendid, and you are the first woman I have ever met who did not want something from me. I had imagined all women to be leeches by their very nature, but you are not. If you were, you would not have tried to leave today."

"And you would not have proposed," she said, with a hint of a smile.

"I would not." He could not help returning the smile. "Miss Holt... Rowena, I cannot promise you love. I can only offer you respect and friendship, and a willingness to do everything in my power to make you happy, but if you feel a distaste for me personally—"

"No," she said quickly. "It is not personal. I always hoped, you see, that one day there would be a man who loved me and whom I could love in return. If I marry you, I surrender all possibility of a marriage of mutual love."

"As do I," he said softly. "The moment I received the letter summoning me to Staineybank, I knew I would have to marry and soon. I would not have the leisure to fall in love. And now that I have seen the sort of women who will be offered to me as potential duchesses, I am even more determined to have none of them. You are far, far above them, Miss Holt, and I beg you to save me from a life shackled to a daughter of the nobility."

She laughed. "May I think about it, Mr Merrington... Richard? It is such a momentous decision to make. Marriage always is, but this is more momentous than most. Let me sleep on it, and I shall give you an answer tomorrow."

And with that he had to be content.

***

Rowena retreated to her room, and methodically changed into a morning gown. It was at least five years old, with two stains that she had never entirely eradicated and a badly repaired tear on one sleeve, but it hardly mattered now.

Georgie crept in, still in her travelling clothes. Seeing Rowena's gown, she said, "I take it we're staying, then."

"Until tomorrow. I shall give him my answer then."

"There can only be one answer, surely? The choice is between unimaginable wealth and status with a pleasant, undemanding husband or a lifetime of poverty and servitude, and possible destitution. How can you even hesitate?"

Rowena smiled. "Is he pleasant and undemanding? We do not know him very well."

"Well, I like him," Georgie said robustly. "I like him a lot better than that stuck-up viscount who made sheep's eyes at you last night."

"He was a dreadful flirt, it is true."

"Exactly. He ignored the Merrington sisters as much as he could, and flirted with you, which is rude, isn't it? And if he wanted an unmarried young lady to flirt with, he should have chosen the duchess's sister. None of Lord Yeldon's family said a word to her, did you notice? Just because she's plain and shy. I think they all behaved disgracefully. Whereas your Mr Merrington has beautiful manners. Well, if you don't want him, tell him that I'd be happy to take him, and live in luxury for the rest of my life."

There was a timid knock on the door, and the duchess's head appeared. "May I come in? I should like to talk to you."

"Of course, your grace."

"Oh, please, call me Lily. Forgive my impertinence, Miss Holt, but I cannot bear to see you harried into this marriage if you had rather not. I know you will think that you cannot refuse, but I want you to know that you can, if you find the prospect distasteful to you. If you prefer to be a governess, I can find you a good position — that is one of the advantages of being a duchess, you see, that people fall over themselves to oblige you. So you need not marry merely for security or a good home."

"You are very kind," Rowena said. "I think perhaps you speak from the heart on the question of being pushed into marriage."

The duchess blushed. "It is true... I *was* pushed... the advantages for the family, you see. And... it has not been easy. Not that Richard... *my* Richard, that is, is unkind or anything of that nature, but I hate this great mausoleum of a house, and to be honest, I hate being a duchess. I was never raised to it, and I do not think you were either. So if you wish to refuse, I will make sure you do not suffer by it. That is all."

"How sweet you are!" Rowena cried. "And I do feel for you most sincerely, for your situation has been hard. But *my* Richard is not at all like yours."

"He is young," the duchess said sadly.

"Indeed, he is young and quick of mind and sensible. He has a delightful sense of humour, too."

"Does he?" the duchess said, eyebrows raised.

"It is subtle, but indeed he does. And of course I cannot refuse him. I will never have a better offer, after all, and being a wife is a thousand times better than being a governess. So tomorrow, I shall thank Mr Merrington for the honour he does me and agree to be his wife."

8: A Walk In The Gardens

Richard slept well, as always. Tomorrow his life might change in a dramatic way, or it might not, but he had spent most of his life waiting for his future to be settled, so he wasted no energy on agonising over it. She would accept or she would not, and lying awake fretting would not change that by one iota.

When he awoke, however, he was restless. It was too early to summon Weston, so he shrugged himself into some old clothes and went to find a door into the garden. Greenery would soothe his nerves a little.

Nerves? Yes, he was nervous. He had never proposed marriage before and even though it had happened almost on a whim, he could not be indifferent as to the outcome. He very much wanted Rowena as his wife, he realised, and not merely to save him from the unappealing daughters of earls. He wanted her ease in company, her sharp mind, her good sense.

And she was beautiful… he felt a twinge of regret that he was not handsome enough to be a good match for her.

Once again, he set out for the shrubbery to hide away amidst its great, tall bushes, but once again he fell short of his destination. For there at the fountain, silent at this hour, sat Rowena. She looked up and smiled at him. Such a smile! And perhaps he would see it every day… But there was no point thinking about that yet.

Was it an invitation? He could not be sure.

"I beg your pardon, Miss Holt. Allow me to withdraw and leave you to your meditation."

"Please stay," she said. "I should like to talk to you, if I may."

As he walked towards her, he was conscious of a spasm of fear. Was this to be a rejection after all? How would he cope with that?

"I have been thinking about the difficulties of your position, Mr Merrington," she said, as soon as he sat down on the bench beside her. "How awkward your life has been! The duchess explained a little of the duke's history — the three wives, the four sons who survived long enough to be baptised. And in all that time, you veered between being the heir and not being the heir. Being a duke, ultimately, or being an untitled gentleman."

"The duke had a younger brother for a long time, so when my father was a boy, there was the distinct possibility that he would marry and secure the succession. But he never did, and when he died, we moved a little closer to the title."

"And this latest child lived longer than any of the others. Six years! You must have thought your fate was settled."

"To be honest, I never thought about it at all," he said. "I simply went on with my life as seemed good to me at the time. If the duke had ever taken an interest in me, perhaps it might have hung over me more acutely. When I was ten or eleven, and thinking about my education — should I go to Eton or Harrow, and perhaps Oxford or Cambridge, in time, or was I content with the tutelage I received from the local clergyman? — my father sat me down and explained his own view on the matter of the dukedom. He had never let it affect his life, and he wanted me to follow the same policy. *'If the duke desires you to be educated to whatever degree he deems suitable for a possible heir, then he should see to it, but if he leaves it to us, then we may do as we please.'* And so I have. If I had ever fallen in love, the inheritance would have become a consideration, but as I have not, I can honestly say that the question of whether I became a duke did not affect me in the slightest."

"But now that you know that you will, your comfortable life has been quite overturned."

He gave the slightest shrug of one shoulder. "It is as God decrees. There is no use in repining."

"How easy-going you are! But there is a question I should like to ask you, if I may."

"Of course."

She turned and looked at him with those clear, grey eyes, her gaze fixed on him. Such eyes! It was as if she could see directly into his soul. "Mr Merrington, you made your offer yesterday on impulse, but perhaps upon reflection you have thought better of the idea. If that is so—"

"No!" he burst out. "No, indeed I have not. Have you any reason to doubt my sincerity on the point?"

"I have not, but I should not wish you to feel yourself irrevocably bound by a spur of the moment declaration."

"You may be quite easy on that head. In fact, the more I consider the idea, the more it pleases me. But what of you? Have you reached a decision yet or do you require more time?"

"I have never required time to reach a decision," she said with a little smile. "To be a duchess or to be a governess? Well now, let me think about that..."

"Ah," he said, chagrined. "It is too good an offer to refuse, I suppose."

"I shall certainly never receive a better one, but that does not mean that I have any reservations about accepting it. I have always wanted to marry and have children, and now I shall. It is not a love match, but you said we have an affinity, and I believe that to be true. You also said that you would respect me, and that is an acceptable substitute for affection. The rest of it — living in Staineybank and being a duchess, in time — well, I shall grow accustomed, and it reassures me that all this is new to you, too. So I thank you for the honour you do me, sir, and I accept your most obliging offer with humble gratitude."

"I am so pleased!" he said, reaching out to take her gloved hand. "We shall deal very well together, I am certain of it."

She smiled at him, but said, "I only hope the duke is not too disappointed with your choice. He made the best of it yesterday, but I think he was rather dumbfounded."

"And yet, over the port last night, he talked at great length of his pleasure at having the living image of his dead wife in his home. I assure you, he is well reconciled to the prospect, although I should warn you that he is set on having us married by bishop's licence before the end of the week."

To his surprise, she laughed. "There is no reason to delay, is there?"

"Wedding clothes? Although the duke said that Cousin Hester will organise something for you, and no doubt she will. She organises everything else in this house. Still, it is a big change in your circumstances. Do you not want a little time to get used to the idea?"

"Did you have time to get used to the idea of living here as the heir?"

He chuckled. "Your point is well made. But Rowena," and he took her hand in both of his, "there is no need to rush into it. A betrothal of three months is very common, or even a month, for the banns to be read. If you wish for that, I will undertake to tell the duke."

"You are very good." The grey eyes drew him into their mysterious depths again. Such beautiful eyes! "But let the duke have his bishop's licence, if it pleases him."

"Then... forgive me if this is too personal a matter for you, but I would have no ambiguity on the point. We are expected to provide the next heir, but there is no need to commence our efforts immediately. I should be very happy to give you two or three months to accustom yourself to your new position before I come to your bed, if you would prefer that."

She blushed a little, and the eyes were lowered. "How kind you are! But that is the entire purpose of this marriage, is it not, to produce an heir? In which case, the sooner the better."

"It shall be just as you wish," he said gravely, but inside his heart leapt. There was no missishness about her at all. What a wife she would be! He was a very lucky man.

***

Rowena spent three days in a whirlwind of dress fittings and preparations. She was moved from the room she had shared with Georgie to a room connected to Richard's study, with a large dressing room rapidly filling up with garments. Cousin Hester proved every bit as resourceful as expected, scavenging spare gowns from every lady in the house, with the sole exception of Richard's mother, whose elaborate confections dripping with lace were wildly unsuitable for a new bride, even one destined to be a duchess in time. Expert seamstresses took over an unused room, filled it with bales of silk and muslin and cotton, not to mention ribbons and lace, and set to work refurbishing the donated gowns and creating many more. Hat boxes arrived, filled with delicious confections of chip straw and feathers, along with boxes of gloves, stockings, shawls and parasols.

Richard went off with Mr Hammond to Lichfield to obtain a licence from the bishop, returning the next day. Then he spent a whole day shut away with the duke and several attorneys.

And then on Saturday, Rowena rose early, donned one of her new gowns, with a spencer and matching bonnet, and was driven the two miles to the parish church. By nine in the morning, she had become Mrs Richard Merrington, with a plain gold band on her finger and her marriage lines tucked into her reticule, emerging from church to find half the village gathered to cheer and throw rice, word having spread rapidly. Even a few farmers in their smocks had come in from the fields to wish them well.

Back at Staineybank, all the servants lined up to greet their return, the indoor servants on the steps, and the gardeners and grooms on the drive. Gravely, the duke introduced them all to both Rowena and Richard, and as each one was named, the women bobbed curtsies and the men bowed respectfully.

Breakfast was a more extensive spread than usual, with wine and champagne to drink as well as coffee and chocolate, and the cook had found time to make a wedding cake. There was a general air of celebration, and even the duchess and her sister, still in full black, smiled and drank the newlyweds' health.

After breakfast, as everyone began to disperse about their usual activities, Richard said to Rowena, "What should you like to do this morning,

Mrs Merrington? Do you want to see over the house? Or a walk in the gardens, perhaps?"

"I am supposed to have more dress fittings," she said, with a rueful smile.

He pulled a face. "Ugh. How dull for your wedding day. Might you not enjoy a respite for a while?"

"A walk in the gardens sounds lovely."

She fetched a bonnet to shade her face, but it was too warm a day for a coat or gloves. She wondered how men coped with the heavy wool coats and waistcoats they wore, winter and summer alike. A muslin gown was blissfully comfortable in hot weather.

At first, they wandered about the *parterre* admiring the symmetry, Rowena enjoying the luxury of a man's arm to support her, but before too long they found themselves approaching the fountain, water sparkling in the air.

"Oh, how lovely! The fountain is working again," she cried.

"I asked for it to be started early today," he said.

"Thank you! I love this place, but it is so much pleasanter when the water is moving. Look how it catches the sun!"

"Should you care to sit and watch it for a while?"

She agreed to it at once. How thoughtful he was! Perhaps in the days and years to come he would forget these tiny courtesies, but it was delightful for a rectory daughter to be treated as if she were a proper lady.

For a while they sat in comfortable silence, she watching the fountain, and he, when she happened to glance at him, watching her. She sighed, a sigh of pure pleasure, for her life had changed so much for the better, and the gardens were by no means the least of it. But there was one anxiety in her mind.

"I hope you will not object if Mrs Hastings stays on for a little while longer," she said. "It is a great comfort to me to have an old friend near me when so many momentous changes are underway."

"And you are amongst strangers, too," he said. "Yes, even I am a stranger to you, so of course Mrs Hastings may stay as long as she wishes. Forever, if that is what you both want."

"You are too good! I had not even considered that."

"Certainly you will want her with you for a few weeks yet, at least. As a married woman, she will be able to advise you if you have any questions or concerns."

Rowena chuckled. "Oh yes, I have had the talk from her."

"The talk?"

"What to expect tonight. Also from the duchess, and from your mother, which was very sweet of her."

"Oh." Amusingly, he blushed a little. "Actually, I have had the talk myself, from the duke. A very extensive talk."

"Do men have the talk, too? I always thought a man was born knowing what to do."

He burst out laughing. "No, I assure you! One picks up the basics, of course. My tutor had some very interesting books in his collection, but until one attempts to put such information into practice, so to speak, a little advice is always welcome. Or a very great deal of advice, in the duke's case. He has had much experience in such matters, and he attempted to impart all of it to me at once. My head is spinning."

"Mine, too," she said, suddenly shy. "But I expect we will muddle through somehow."

"I expect we will," he said, smiling down at her.

He reached for her hand and lifted it gently to his lips. For a moment, looking into those shining brown eyes she could almost imagine that there was more than courtesy and respect between them. It was a little like being loved, and just for those few seconds she was slightly breathless, wondering if perhaps he would lean nearer and—

Abruptly, he let go of her hand. "I have something for you," he said, reaching into a pocket. "I hope you will like it."

He laid a small oblong package in her hand, wrapped in silk and tied with a narrow ribbon.

"Oh. Thank you!" Gingerly she unwrapped it to reveal a small leather box. Inside, a string of small diamonds, the sunlight producing flashes of brilliant light from them, so that she gasped. *"Oh!* Oh my! They are... oh, Richard, I have never had anything so beautiful in my life. Thank you so much!"

"I am so glad you like them. It is only a token, but I could not let the day pass unmarked, since I have had no opportunity to buy you a betrothal present. Lichfield was not well endowed with jewellery shops, but it was the best I could do. I shall buy you something finer in London. Oh, and there is this, too."

The hand went into the pocket again, and produced a purse which he laid in her lap.

"What is this?" she said wonderingly, feeling the weight of it against her legs.

"This quarter's allowance. Your pin money. One hundred and twenty-five pounds. That is to last you until Michaelmas so try not to spend it all at once."

"I do not understand. Where did this come from?"

"Well now, that is a difficult question to answer. I suppose, to be very precise, it came from the duke's safe, since I have not sufficient funds here to cover the amount, but in the future, it will come directly from me. It is all specified in your settlement."

Rowena felt as if she had strayed into a dream. Pin money? A settlement? "But that would be *five hundred pounds a year!* Do you expect me to spend that much on gowns... or jewels?"

"Not jewels, no. It is for your husband to provide such things — the real jewellery, at least. There is family jewellery, too. You may use any piece which the duchess does not wish to wear. But gowns? Yes, all your clothes, and whatever else you want to buy. Your pin money is yours to do with as you please." He laughed at her astonished face. "You had no idea, had you? Did you never think to ask about your settlement?"

"But how can I have a settlement? I have no dowry!"

"I should be a very remiss husband if I married you without making a settlement. What did you imagine the attorneys were doing here all day yesterday?"

"Your will?" she said hesitantly, guessing, for she had not thought about the question at all.

"Yes, I made a new will, to make provision for you, as well as my mother and sisters, if they remain unmarried. And a settlement for you. The duke has settled ten thousand pounds on you as dowry, which comes to me as your husband, and the interest comes to you as your pin money. And if I should die before you, then you will have Leahollow, both the house and the income. If the dukedom passes through me to our son, then it will be yours for your lifetime and then revert to the ducal estate, but if the dukedom passes in the present duke's line, then—"

"But has he not given up all thought of that? The duchess is to return to Cheshire."

"So he says, but he might change his mind, or it might transpire that his younger brother married and sired an heir, who knows? It is important to take account of all possibilities. In any event, if the dukedom does *not* pass through my line, and I predecease you, then Leahollow will be yours absolutely, to dispose of as you see fit after your death. The income is only around twelve hundred a year, but it should be enough to live on, with care, even if there are several children to support."

"And your mother and sisters," she said.

He burst out laughing. "Yes, I am afraid there is no getting rid of them, and they are inclined to be extravagant, if given the least opening. I had to watch the pennies very carefully. Shall you mind if they are still around?"

Rowena shook her head. "I never had sisters, so it will be a treat for me to have four of them."

Richard looked rueful. "A treat? For you, perhaps, but I have never known what to do with them."

"Ah, but you are a man, and therefore have no interest in bonnets. I assure you, I consider it a rare treat to have so many opinions to consult on the matter of bonnets, especially now that I can afford several new bonnets a year."

"I concede the point. Oh, I hear voices approaching. Are you minded to be sociable or shall we sneak away to the shrubbery?"

Lowering her voice, she said, "Let us sneak away."

"Quickly, then."

He helped her to her feet, and hand in hand they slipped away towards the shrubbery, giggling like children.

9: North And South Again

Just two hours after the wedding breakfast had ended, a carriage pulled up at the front door, disgorging a family draped in deepest black, arrived to offer condolences. A month having passed since the death of the young Marquess of Losseter, they had ventured forth to see if the ducal family had recovered sufficiently from their grief to receive visitors. To their bemusement, they found themselves instead making the first bridal visit, and regaled with wedding cake and champagne.

Richard watched them with amusement, shedding tears with the duchess on one side of the room, then offering smiles and well-wishes to Rowena on the other. To the duke, they had no idea what to say. Were condolences or congratulations more in order?

While the ladies were busy with the bereaved mother and the bride, the father came to shake Richard's hand.

"Very glad to meet you at last, Merrington," he said. "I have advised Brinshire these many years that you should be brought into the fold, as it were, just in case, especially after your father died." He glanced across to where the Merrington ladies were giggling with the visiting daughters. "So much feminine influence is not ideal for any man, least of all one destined for high estate. But there, Brinshire was always one to go his own way."

"Indeed, and I had an excellent tutor who was as much a father to me as anyone could be."

"Good, good. Glad to see you are doing your duty at once. Who is she, your wife? A family connection? She is very like the portrait in the library."

"She is the very image of the duke's first duchess, the former Lady Caroline Bucknell, but we know of no connection to my wife," Richard said. "She is... or rather was Miss Holt from Oxford. Her father was rector at a parish just outside the town, and her mother was a Miss Winthrop from Northumberland. Nothing to do with the Bucknells, at least nothing acknowledged."

"Ah, yes. An irregular connection. That could well be so, although I never heard of any amongst the Bucknells, not in that generation, anyway. I know the present Duke of Camberley well, and he likes to boast that his family is less licentious than most. Now, Brinshire — ha! A very colourful history there. You should ask him about it some time."

"I have heard something of it," Richard said drily, remembering the talk.

"It would not surprise me if he has scattered by-blows up and down the country. But the Bucknells? Not a whisper."

"That may only mean that they are better at covering up their mistakes."

"Ha! Possibly so. Well, I wish you joy, young man. Time for me to drag the ladies away."

After a brief respite on Sunday, Monday saw the start of the onslaught of morning calls. Hardly an hour went by between breakfast and the dressing bell when there were no visitors sipping sherry and devouring cakes in the White Drawing Room. Even if there happened to be a lull, Rowena spent every spare minute on fittings for gowns, pelisses, bonnets, gloves and even riding habits, although she had not ridden for some years. Richard felt he hardly saw her except in the bedroom, where conversation was not greatly on their minds.

As for his own time, he had finally been permitted to look at the accounts, and found them disquieting. It was not the numbers that disturbed him, for the totals were reassuringly high and he was pleased to see that the duke's income was in excess of twenty thousand pounds a year, and his expenditure considerably less. But in the detail, he was uneasy. Even with the far greater breadth of the duke's estates, his ability with numbers and analysing a chess board gave him the power to see patterns even in so much information.

When he mentioned his concerns to the duke, however, they were brushed aside.

"Pyott has been with me for years, and Monk too, and even if one of them were diddling me, the other would know about it."

"I would not go so far as to say that there is any diddling going on, but there is something not quite right about it, all the same. Have you anyone who might look over the accounts — an outsider, who would give you an independent opinion?"

"Nonsense, boy! I would not insult Pyott or Monk by bringing someone in to check up on them. What would you know about managing the sort of operations that go on under my aegis anyway? What is your little estate worth? Two thousand a year?"

"Twelve hundred pounds."

"There you are, then. My income is ten times yours."

"Twenty, sir. Your income is almost twenty times mine."

"Ah! Is it so? Then you cannot possibly understand the complexities of it as Pyott does. When it is yours, you can do what you like, you know, but until then, do not be casting aspersions on good honest men. I cannot abide that sort of underhand nastiness. You concentrate on that wife of yours, that is your principal concern now."

"I would if I ever saw her," he muttered.

The duke chuckled. "You see her in bed, and what else is needed?"

To Richard, these words echoed round his head powerfully. What else *was* needed to make Rowena happy? What was needed to make him happy, for that matter?

On Sunday morning, he woke early, Rowena still peacefully sleeping beside him. He smiled as he looked at her, the neat plait with which she habitually started the night unravelled and spread over the pillow. Marriage had turned out better than he had hoped, in some ways, but Staineybank was suffocating him. The duke's restrictions and the deluge of callers were bad enough, but his mother and sisters were still there, and showing no sign of leaving. The duchess, who also showed no sign of leaving, liked them, and that was enough to secure their favour with the duke.

When Rowena woke, she smiled at him sleepily. "Have you been awake long?"

"A little while. I have been thinking — would you like to go on a wedding tour?"

"Oh — can we?"

"If we want to. It is very common to take a month or so to visit relations in distant parts of the country, or simply to have time away from the pressures of normal life. I suspect we could both do with that. We would take Mrs Hastings with us, of course."

"How lovely! But where would we go? I have no relations, and yours are here, so what did you have in mind?"

"I thought we might go to Northumberland and see if we can find out something about your mother. It is a big county, but someone must know the Winthrops. We will find where she lived eventually."

Rowena sat up abruptly, rearranging the pillows to prop herself up, her face alight with excitement. "But I know where she lived! It was a tiny village called West Belcroft, nothing but a single street, a church and an inn — the White Swan. The house she lived in was Holly Cottage. She talked about it so much, I can almost picture it in my mind — the holly tree by the gate, the honeysuckle round the door, the orchard at the side of the house with a swing where she used to play. And geese — there was a pond and they had ducks and geese. Oh, I should so much like to see it!"

"Then we will," he said, with a glow of satisfaction. He had done something to make her happy!

***

The journey to Northumberland took five days, which passed in a pleasant haze of swift attention at toll gates and faultless service at posting houses, facilitated by the duke's coat of arms on the carriage doors. Richard, Rowena and Mrs Hastings enjoyed the utmost comfort in the duke's newest travelling carriage, while the luggage and servants were ensconced in a capacious second carriage.

Richard had no complaint about the company, either, finding that Mrs Hastings was just as agreeable a companion as his wife, the three soon being entirely on first name terms. After a good dinner each evening accompanied by a little wine and a great deal of wide-ranging conversation, he and Rowena generally played chess while Georgie sewed or read or dozed by the fire. It was a delight to him to find not one but two women who could talk about subjects other than themselves, their apparel and their various engagements, and who wanted nothing from him.

It was also a pleasure to have money and to spare. Not only did Richard have his own modest income from Leahollow and a generous allowance as well, but before departure the duke had pressed into his hand a purse heavy with golden guineas, together with letters of introduction to banks in case he needed more, and more letters of introduction to various friends in the north, including the Marquess of Carrbridge and the Duke of Dunmorton.

"Do you wish me to call upon these people?" he had said, appalled at the prospect of paying courtesy visits to distinguished gentlemen and peers in several counties.

"No, no, but if you should encounter any difficulty or need help, they will be delighted to oblige you, just as I would do for them and their kin if the situation were reversed. Any gentleman would help out another gentleman. You are connected to the nobility now, you know, and the aristocracy looks after its own."

"It is a giant club, is it not?" Richard said. "You all know each other."

"Oh, more than that — we are all related to each other. I married a daughter of the Duke of Camberley, he married a daughter of the Duke of Dunmorton, while he married a daughter of the Duke of Wedhampton, and so it goes on."

"Ah. And I broke the chain. I beg your pardon, sir."

"Do you regret it?" the duke said, eyes twinkling.

"Not for one second."

The duke chuckled. "Good. Eyebrows will be raised by it, make no mistake, but take no notice of that. Rowena is from perfectly respectable stock. Eyebrows were raised when I married Lily, too, but as God is my witness, Richard, she has done me so much good. Such a lovely girl, in ways as well as looks, and although it was deeply selfish of me, in the end she will do well out of it. When I am gone, she will still be young enough to marry again and have more children, and her jointure is hers absolutely, so she can marry where she pleases next time. A fine, handsome fellow, I hope, who will cherish her as she deserves — as I have tried to do. Ah, all this talk of wives makes me maudlin. Go on, get off with you, boy."

On the fifth day, Rowena sat upright in the carriage, gazing avidly through the windows at the passing fields and tiny villages. Richard delighted in her excitement. He had not realised just how much she longed to see the place where her mother had grown up. He had suggested it almost on a whim, because he himself was curious as to how she had come by her extraordinary resemblance to the Lady Caroline Bucknell, but he was thrilled to be bringing her so much pleasure.

They passed through several undistinguished villages after leaving the turnpike, but eventually they arrived at the one they sought — West Belcroft. It was, as he had expected, just as undistinguished as the others, the street lined with low cottages and a few larger dwellings, all in the local grey stone with slate roofs.

"There is the inn just ahead," Richard said, twisting to peer through the window. "I suggest we stop there and bespeak rooms for tonight. Then, when we have discovered where Holly Cottage is located, we can walk there before dinner."

"The inn has changed its name," Rowena said. "It is the Pack Horse now, not the White Swan."

"It will do well enough, whatever its name," Richard said. "It looks respectable, anyway."

All three descended from the carriage, and were ushered inside by a bowing innkeeper.

"Are you Mr Pride?" Rowena said eagerly.

"No, mum. Randall's my name."

"Ah, in my mother's day, it was Mr Pride, but that was many years ago."

The innkeeper looked bemused. "Been Randalls here ever since t'inn were built, mum."

It was Rowena's turn to look bemused, and Richard stepped in quickly to solicit accommodation for themselves, their servants and the postilions and horses. By the time all was done, he learnt that the ladies had already been led away to the inn's only private parlour. There he found Rowena pacing back and forth.

"This place has never been the White Swan, Richard, never! And there is no Holly Cottage, according to the maid, nor does she know of anyone called Winthrop. What does it mean?"

Certain obvious answers rose to his mind, but he said only, "Perhaps you mistook the name of the village? Is there an East Belcroft, perhaps?"

"I could not have mistaken the name! Mama talked of it so many times."

Georgie said diffidently, "The maid said there's a house called Hollydale in the next village, so perhaps—"

"No!" Rowena said. "She lived in *this* village."

"How far is it to the next village?" Richard said neutrally.

"The maid described it as *'a mile or a little more',*" Georgie said, "which probably means two or three miles."

"Let us bespeak dinner for… shall we say two hours from now?" Richard said. "Then we can walk to Hollydale and see if it bears any resemblance to Holly Cottage. I should be glad of an excuse to stretch my legs anyway. We have been cooped up in that carriage far too much."

But Hollydale was a disappointment, too. It was as far as it could be from the picturesque cottage Rowena had envisaged, being a vast Tudor building on several floors, all mullioned windows and great tall chimneys.

"Shall we knock and enquire?" Richard said.

Rowena turned amazed eyes on him. "You mean, just walk up to a house where we know no one and say, *'Excuse me, but do you happen to know of a Jenny Winthrop, who once lived in these parts?'*"

"Yes, why not?" he said, with a quick laugh. "We are a future duke and duchess, after all, and his grace made it clear to me that we have the entrée to any gentleman's house where we might need help. And we do need help, would you not agree? The puzzle of your ancestry has become even more puzzling, and it may be that these people, strangers though they may be, hold the key to unravelling the mystery. We have come all this way to find where your mother lived, Rowena. Let us not give up at the first check."

So they walked up the drive to the house, and Richard handed over his card to the very grand butler, explaining that he was heir to the Duke of Brinshire, currently engaged in tracing a distant relation in the area, and would be much obliged if the master or mistress of the house would be so gracious as to receive him. And just as the duke had predicted, the butler ushered them into a well-appointed drawing room, where the lady of the house sat with her daughter. Within a few minutes, her husband and two sons appeared from some male fastness, refreshments were provided and they were received as graciously as if this were a morning call in Mayfair.

They had, however, no information to impart. They had never heard of Holly Cottage, nor of Jenny Winthrop, or any Winthrop at all. Even when the housekeeper was applied to, in case the servants might know of such a person, the answer was still negative. So they left none the wiser, although full of wine and cake, and were driven back to the inn in their hosts' carriage to spare them the walk.

Rowena was silent throughout dinner, but after the servants had left, she burst out, "What can it mean? Did Mama lie to me, and if so, why?"

"We cannot know, at this point," Richard said cautiously. "Any explanations we might dream up would be nothing but speculation. Do you have anything of your mother's? Any papers, letters, jewellery, that sort of thing?"

"There is a small box of her things still in the trunk I left behind at Georgie's house. Her baptism certificate, for one thing."

"Then let us go there and look at it, and see what else might be tucked away in that box. We may find a clue that you would not have understood before, but which will mean something now."

Slowly, Rowena nodded, but the sadness on her face did not lift.

***

The journey south was less pleasant. The service they received was just as attentive, but Rowena was out of spirits and Mrs Hastings was sensitive to her friend's mood, so for long hours they sat in silence as the carriage bumped and swayed its way to Oxfordshire. They had planned to go directly to Georgie's cottage, but Richard had arranged a surprise with the postilions, and so shortly after noon, they drew up outside the small parish church of St Jude's. The footman opened the door and let down the steps, and the three friends descended to the road.

"Go on to the inn just across the green," Richard told the postilions. "Bait the horses and wait for us there."

The two carriages rumbled away, raising a choking dust.

Richard turned to Rowena, who was staring pale-faced at the church and the pretty rectory alongside it. "Why have you brought me here?" she said, her tone flat.

"I thought after the disappointment of Northumberland, you would enjoy seeing a place with happier memories." Then, puzzled at her lack of response, he went on, "It is the right place, is it not? St Jude's, where your father was rector?"

"It is."

"Then it is where you grew up, where your mother talked to you about Holly Cottage. I thought... I hoped it would please you."

"You could have asked me."

"I beg your pardon," he said humbly. "I meant it as a pleasant surprise."

"Well, it is not," she spat with a vehemence that shocked him. "Oh, I cannot bear it! It is too much, entirely too much!"

To his horror, great tears rolled down her cheeks. "Rowena, I—"

"This was such a mistake... I should have known... I ought to have realised it was too good to be true."

"Your mother?" he hazarded.

"No — *you!* Such a mistake! Oh, I wish I had never married you!"

And so saying, she half ran down the road away from him, leaving Richard stunned and despairing.

10: St Jude's

Richard stood as if turned to stone, Rowena's words echoing in his head like the tolling of a funeral bell.

'I wish I had never married you.'

Did she hate him so much? Yet she had seemed to be happy until West Belcroft and the mysterious non-existence of Holly Cottage. She had been subdued all the way south. But this... this was different. Her own home and the memories of her happy childhood had brought home to her exactly what she had lost by marrying without love. Yes, she had secured her own future, but she had given up all chance of a marriage of true affection. And perhaps there had been someone, a man she could not marry for one reason or another. Perhaps he was unable to support a wife, or perhaps he was already married. Or perhaps as she pined for him, he had never noticed her.

No, surely not. She was so beautiful that every man must notice her.

"Richard..." Georgie diffidently tugged at his sleeve. "Won't you go after her?"

He dragged his thoughts with difficulty back to the present situation. Should he go after her? "No, she does not want me."

"Then I'll go, but she's in no state to drive further today. Will you go and take rooms at that inn down there? Just for tonight. Tomorrow she may be well enough to get to Oakfordham."

"Inn. Rooms. Yes," he muttered, but without moving.

Georgie gave him a little push in the right direction. "Go on! I must chase after Rowena before she's quite out of sight."

"Inn..." He looked up and around, saw the inn sign just a little way down the road and took a step in that direction. "Inn... rooms." Another step, then another. Gradually, the inn neared and he slowed to a crawl and then stopped altogether.

After a moment, Weston came out of what must be the common room. "Sir? Do you want the horses put to again?"

Richard licked his lips. "Rooms..." he croaked.

"Oh, are we staying? Are you quite well, sir? You look very pale. Come and sit down. This place is quite respectable." Then, after a hesitation, he went on, "Shall I see to the rooms for you, sir?"

"Yes, do that, if you please. I just need... to sit down for a bit."

His knees were almost buckling under him, he realised. Weston gently led him to a bench in a shady spot, where he sat, eyes closed. A pot boy came out with a tankard of ale for him, but he waved it away. Ale would not mend what was broken inside him. He knew that something was broken, or it would not hurt so much. His heart, possibly. Just three weeks married and already he could not imagine life without Rowena. He had been so happy... had thought she was happy, too, but it was all a lie, nothing but a lie.

'I wish I had never married you.'

God help him, how was he to live the rest of his life without her? But he must! If she hated him so much, then he must do whatever it took to bring her peace and contentment with a situation so unbearable to her. He would go away... no, he was the duke's heir, and he could hardly leave Staineybank now. But he could provide a home for her elsewhere. That was it... they could live separate lives, and she would be happy... as happy as she could be. Without him.

He bowed his head, and let despair consume him.

Sometime later, he could not tell how much, Weston came back. "I have secured two bedrooms and a parlour for you, sir, and suitable accommodation for the rest of us. Will you come up to the parlour now? It is a little public here. The landlord is sending up food and wine, and wishes to discuss dinner with you. Or I could order for you, if you like, sir?"

"Yes, do that, if you would."

He allowed Weston to lead him to the parlour, which was much like any other parlour in a small rural inn away from the main turnpikes. It was clean, however, and a jug of dried flowers on the hearth spoke of a degree of care. Weston pressed a glass of something into his hand.

"Drink, sir. You'll feel a bit better with some wine inside you. The bedrooms are directly opposite, across the corridor, the one on the left is the best room in the house, for you and Mrs Merrington. Mrs Hastings will have the other. That's the ladies arriving now, sir. Do you want to show them the rooms?"

He shook his head. "You do it, Weston."

"Very good, sir."

Richard strained his ears to hear something — anything — from Rowena, but there was only the rumble of Weston's voice from the corridor outside, and the sound of doors opening and closing. A little while later, footsteps on the stairs and an occasional thump suggested the luggage was being brought up. Inn workers crept in with platters of food, and crept out again, all too aware of the ongoing crisis.

He did not care. His world had come crashing down around his ears, and it mattered not who knew of the disaster. His mind spun on the two points — what had he done wrong? And was there any way he could put it right?

Georgie came in, and his head shot up at once. "How is she?"

"Still weeping. I've left Mary sitting with her. I have good news and bad."

"Tell me the bad first."

"The landlord recognised me."

"Oh. You used to visit Rowena?"

"No, I lived here myself. They will recognise Rowena, too, eventually, when she emerges from her handkerchief. This will feed all sorts of rumours."

"It cannot be helped. What was the good news?"

"Not so much news as a word of encouragement. Rowena is in a somewhat unsettled state at the moment. I don't think you should take her words as being a true reflection of her sentiments."

"Georgie, you are an optimist, but she said very clearly and unambiguously that she wished she had never married me. Try as I might, I cannot interpret that as anything other than a disaster."

"Do you want to go and talk to her?"

He shook his head. "I would only distress her again. If she wishes to talk to me, I am here, or she can ask for me to go to her, but I will not force myself on her ever again. You must share with her tonight, and I will take the other room, and tomorrow, if she wishes, I will go away. Or she can have the carriage and go wherever she wishes. To your house or... anywhere she wants. My house in Norwich is empty, so if she wishes to live apart—"

"Richard—"

"— she can go there. It is still fully staffed. Whatever she wants, she can have. Will you tell her all this? Tell her I want her to be... perhaps not happy, if that prospect is lost forever, but at least at peace and free to live her life without me. Will you tell her, Georgie? And tell her I am sorry... for everything."

After a hesitation, Georgie nodded. "I'll tell her, if she ever stops weeping."

The afternoon and evening drifted away. Richard sat unmoving, lost in sorrow and regret. The servants came in and out, laying out the dinner, then clearing it away later virtually untouched. Georgie came in, filled a plate for Rowena and another for herself, and went away again. At some point, Richard decided savagely that he might at least get drunk and perhaps that would numb the pain a little and help him to sleep, but even glass after glass of wine left him sober and miserable.

Weston eventually chased him away to bed, where he lay wakeful, a candle still burning so that he could check his pocket watch for the hour. Twenty to midnight. Five minutes past. A quarter past. Not quite half past. Twenty to one. Five minutes to one. Ten minutes past. Almost half past. The candle sputtered and winked out, leaving the room lit by only a thin shaft of moonlight.

A sound.

He strained his ears... what was it? The inn, not being on a main coach route, was slumbering, the tap room long since fallen silent.

There it was again. A door latch. His own, he guessed. Then a creak of the door opening. One of the servants? A thief? The door creaked shut again, and the latch sounded. Now his visitor was inside the room with him. The intruder crossed the beam of moonlight so that for a second he caught sight of a figure in white, with a long plait falling over one shoulder.

Rowena was in his room! Joy rose up inside him, followed instantly by terror. What did she want? To talk? Was she about to accept his offer to live separately? She drew nearer, nearer, so close he could smell faint traces of her perfume, hear her ragged breathing mingled with the tiniest little sob now and then. She was standing right beside the bed, so close, so unbearably close.

He lay, frozen in fear, to see what she would do. He closed his eyes, praying fervently that this was something good, a reconciliation… and for the strength to endure it if it were not.

The blankets were lifted, and the bed rocked a little as she climbed in, lying down beside him.

His heart soared with happiness. She was here in his bed, her body so near to his that he could feel her warmth. And then, unbelievably, she made his joy complete by rolling onto her side and resting one arm across his chest. With another little sob, and then a long, low sigh, she lay still, and as he listened her breathing slowed and in time he guessed she had fallen asleep.

He smiled in the darkness, wanting to laugh, to cry, to shout to the world that she was back with him, his lovely Rowena was in his arms again, but terrified of waking her. So he lay immobile, grinning inanely, wondering if it were possible to die of happiness. Whatever the morning might bring, he was at peace and gradually, after a long time, his eyes closed again and he slept.

***

Rowena woke with a start, as a carriage arrived at the inn with a great noise of horn-blowing and shouts and clattering of hooves and wheels. For a few seconds, she felt at ease, warm and comfortable in bed, with Richard's slumbering form beside her.

Then she remembered.

St Jude's. The rectory. The overwhelming memories, which had quite crushed her. What had she said and done? She could hardly remember, except that Georgie had told her what Richard had said, that they were to live separately from now on.

Her marriage was over, almost before it had begun.

She sat up abruptly, shaking. Beside her, Richard stirred and opened his eyes. He smiled at her. *Smiled!* Perhaps things were not so desperate after all.

"Good morning," he said, still smiling.

"Is it?"

The smile slipped a little. "I think it is, anyway. You are here with me, so that makes it a good morning for me. Is it not for you?"

He was adjusting the pillows as he spoke, arranging them so that she could lean against them while sitting up, then moving his own likewise.

She could not make sense of it, but she grasped the important point — he was glad she had come to him. "I… yes," was all she could manage.

"Are you feeling better?" he said softly, and the gentle affection in his voice, in his eyes almost undid her. She felt tears, never far below the surface since yesterday, rising up again.

"Oh, Richard!"

She curled into him, one hand clutching at his nightshirt as she wept, and his arms wrapped around her and held her tight. After all the drama of yesterday, she was safe at last.

"Thank you," he murmured into her hair.

"For what?"

"For coming back to me."

"It is my place."

He stiffened, and she knew she had said the wrong thing. Lifting her head and wiping away the tears, she saw such a sorrowful expression there that she quailed.

"I see. So you are just doing your duty," he said, his voice harsh.

"No! No, no, no!" She pushed herself upright, away from him, so that she could see his face more clearly. "I meant only that this is where I belong, with you. It is where I need to be... where I *want* to be. But if you do not want me—"

"Of course I want you! Whatever made you think...? Dearest, there is nothing I want more, but if I make you unhappy—"

"No, not you." *Dearest!* He had called her his dearest. That must mean... surely...?

"Marriage, then. Marriage to me makes you unhappy," he said, his tone a shade softer.

"No!"

"Then why did you say you wished you had never married me?"

She frowned, trying to make sense of his words. "Did I say that?"

He gave a short laugh. "You did! I thought... I assumed you meant it, but... I do not understand. What happened yesterday?"

She sat up a little straighter. "It was seeing the rectory again and realising that all those happy times I remembered, all those memories my mother shared with me of her own childhood — it was nothing but lies, from start to finish. There was no Holly Cottage, no pond with ducks and geese, no nursemaid called Meg, no ever-present and loving mother —

none of it was true. My own mother looked me straight in the eye and lied to me, to her own daughter. And I cannot forgive her, because I am not who I thought I was. I do not know who I am, but I know very clearly that I am not fit to be the wife of a good, honourable man like you. My whole life is a falsehood, Richard, and I cannot bear it!"

"Oh, Rowena, my dear," he murmured, pulling her back into his arms. "As if any of that matters to me. I love you just the way you are."

She went very still, some strange emotion roiling through her. *Love?* Did he dare to speak of love? And did he mean it? So many questions, so many fears and hopes.

"Love?" she whispered.

"I know, it is too soon, is it not?" he said, his dark eyes alight with strange fire. "Far too soon! Three weeks ago tomorrow since we married, and yet... I do not know what else to call it, this terrible darkness that lay on me when I thought I had lost you forever, and the joy when you came to me last night."

"Darkness... yes," she said wonderingly. "When Georgie told me that you wanted us to live apart, I was so crushed—"

"*I* wanted?" he said sharply. "No, never! I thought it was what *you* wanted, since you said... Oh, but we have misunderstood each other horribly, have we not? You do not wish you had never married me, and I do not wish us to live apart." He gave a little laugh. "It is the strangest thing, for I never thought of marriage except as a far distant thing that might happen one day, and never felt any great longing for it. Even when I entered the state of matrimony, it was for the vaguest of reasons — that you were enchanted by the fountain, and you could play chess. Such a flimsy foundation. And yet in less than three weeks of married life, I find that you are quite indispensable to my happiness. Oh, Rowena, let us never again mistake each other so utterly. I am so sorry I ever brought you here and reminded you of your mother's lies... or whatever they were."

"You do not choose to call them lies? What else could they be?"

"A lie is something mischievous, to me. Wicked, even. But I do not think a mother willingly lies to her child, except to protect her from a worse truth. Suppose there was something shameful in her childhood that she wished to forget... a violent father, perhaps, or a neglectful mother. Perhaps she was a foundling, abandoned at birth. We suspect that she may have been illegitimate, so that is possible, is it not? But she does not wish to tell you such a sad tale, so she invents the happy childhood that she wished she had enjoyed herself. That way, she ensures that you, at least, have a loving family life, unshaded by the world's darkness."

"You think, then, that it was a kindness? To protect me?"

"I think it could have been," he said gently. "And if so, you need not fear the memories of the rectory."

"Perhaps," she said slowly. "But it is one thing to protect a child, and another altogether to keep the truth from a grown daughter. When she knew she was dying, that would have been the time to tell me the truth, or to write a letter for me to read when I came of age. She could have left me *something*, some little hint."

"And perhaps she did, but you did not understand it before. So let us go and look through the box of her papers and see what we can find, shall we?"

***

Oakfordham Cottage was a modest labourer's dwelling, with two parlours and a kitchen downstairs, and two bedrooms of equal size above. Georgie's maid of all work, Annie, emerged to greet them with pleasure and surprise, her first words being, "Oh, but there ain't nuffin' but a bit o' bread an' cheese in the 'ouse."

Happily, this proved not to be a problem, for all the neighbours emerged at the sight of the two ducal carriages, and a gentle fight began to be the ones to offer hospitality to the three friends. With good dinners assured for as long as they chose to stay, Rowena left Richard to supervise the unloading of the luggage, negotiate accommodation for the servants with neighbours and pay off the postilions.

Inside, she murmured to Georgie, "You told them about the wedding, I take it? I do not think your friends would be quite so welcoming if it had merely been the two of us. Mrs Childs would have sent round the remains of a pie, perhaps, and Mrs Burnley a pot of soup. Whereas we are to be fed like royalty, by the sound of it."

"Naturally I wrote to tell everyone of your good fortune," Georgie said, smiling. "I'm afraid you'll never be allowed to dine on the remains of a pie ever again. You're going to be a duchess, my dear friend, so you must become accustomed to the whole world falling over itself to accommodate your every whim. And naturally, if a neighbour goes to the trouble of entertaining you in grand style, you must in your turn provide entertainment for your hosts."

"You are not speaking, I collect, of a performance on the pianoforte?"

"What's wanted, my dear unworldly friend, is tales of the ducal family in which you now move. Tales which will be passed around from mouth to mouth and house to house. *'Have you heard?'* they will whisper to each other. *'The Duke of Brinshire's heir stayed in that very cottage and sat at my table and complimented my lamb cutlets.'* They'll want to know all about the duke and duchess, and about Staineybank, and before a se'nnight has passed every word of it will be all over Oxford, and beyond."

"Beyond! Surely not?"

"But certainly, for Mrs Burnley will write to her sister in Manchester, and Mrs Childs to her cousins in Weymouth, and they will write to all their relations. You're a person of the greatest interest now, my dear, so you may as well get used to it. Will Richard mind sleeping under the eaves, do you suppose? He's so easy-going that one imagines he wouldn't complain if asked to sleep in the coal cellar."

"He will not mind, I am sure."

"No, for he's so recently married that he'll scarcely notice the bedroom so long as you're in the bed."

"Georgie!"

She laughed. "Men are simple creatures, Rowena, and easy to please. Oh, but I'm so glad you managed to clear up your differences. He's such a good man — you're very lucky, you know. Luckier than I was, perhaps, for all I loved Henry dearly, so make the most of him."

"I intend to," Rowena said seriously. "I am very aware of my good fortune, Georgie. I had no great expectations for this marriage, and perhaps there will still be bumps in the road ahead, but we will overcome them together." She gave a little laugh. "He is lovely, do you not agree?"

"Of course I do. I'm very jealous!"

They were laughing together when Richard came into the room. "What are you jealous about, Georgie?"

"Never you mind!" Rowena said briskly. "Would the future Duke of Brinshire like to see his room? I regret that it is not quite as spacious as your apartments at Staineybank."

"So long as it has a bed and you, I shall be quite content."

"There you are, you see?" Georgie said triumphantly. "Simple creatures."

The two burst out laughing, and Richard laughed too, shaking his head at them. "Ah, I see, I am the butt of your humour, am I? But I have the most beautiful woman in all England as my charming wife, so I care nothing for your jests."

Georgie sighed sentimentally at this romantic declaration. Rowena, on the other hand, blushed furiously, and decided she was the luckiest woman alive.

11: Marshfields

The next day was Sunday. Rowena was minded to stay quietly at the cottage, but remembering Georgie's words about providing entertainment for the locals, she instead donned one of her most fashionable bonnets and accompanied Richard and Georgie to Mr Child's church. It was not unlike her father's church of St Jude's, but she allowed the familiarity to wash around her unchecked this time. Perhaps, as Richard suggested, her mother's lies were intended to protect her from unpleasantness, to provide her with the image of an idyllic childhood. Or perhaps her mother had been protecting herself, shutting out bad memories by painting a rosier picture. Rowena might never understand the reason.

She was coming to terms with that. Richard's words still rang in her head. *'As if any of that matters to me. I love you just the way you are.'* If it did not matter to him who her mother was, or what her childhood might have been, then it did not matter to Rowena, either. She had enjoyed a happy childhood, and now she was embarking on what she hoped — believed — would be a happy marriage. She would still like to understand her connection to Lady Caroline Bucknell, but even if she never discovered it, she could accept that with equanimity.

After the service, they returned to the cottage for breakfast, well provisioned by the generosity of their friends. Then they turned to the small box that contained all the property that now remained of Jenny Holt née Winthrop.

Rowena brought the box down to the front parlour, and gently turned the key to unlock it. She knew the contents intimately by now. A bundle of letters, some modest jewellery, a prayer book, several exquisitely embroidered handkerchiefs, some drawings of Rowena as a child, her father and the rectory, a miniature showing five unknown people in antiquated dress and finally, right at the bottom, her mother's baptism certificate.

"Hmm. *'Ruth Jane Winthrop, at St Michael's Church in the see of Durham',*" Richard read. "That does sound like Northumberland. But no town or parish is mentioned."

"How curious," Georgie said. "Jane was her middle name, yet she went by Jenny rather than Ruth. But who are these people in the little painting?"

"I have no idea," Rowena said. "I took it out of the frame once to see if there is any paper concealed there with names, but there was nothing."

"This symbol at the top of the frame — that's a coat of arms, isn't it?" Georgie said.

"It could be."

Richard was leafing through the prayer book to see if any long-hidden paper fell out, but set it down, frustrated. "Who are the letters from?"

"A Mrs Lacey. The Laceys are a prominent Oxford family. My mother was sent to her when she was sixteen to be brought out and married off. That is how she ended up marrying an Oxfordshire rector."

"So she knew your grandmother, this Mrs Lacey?"

"Yes, but if you imagine there is some clue in the letters, you are sadly mistaken. You are welcome to read them all, if you wish."

"Have you talked to Mrs Lacey?"

"She has been dead these ten... no, twelve years now. I met her daughter once, but she knew nothing about my mother or any connection. I do not think there is anything to be gleaned from the Laceys."

"Hmm." Richard sighed. He picked up the miniature and squinted at the symbol on the top. "I think this *is* a coat of arms, and I would wager that it is for the Bucknells. After all, we know there must be a connection there somewhere."

"Mr Childs will know," Georgie said. "He has a copy of the Peerage. All the coats of arms are in there, aren't they? When we go there for dinner, he'll look it up for us."

Mr Childs, it turned out, was thrilled with the miniature, producing a magnifying glass and poring over the coat of arms. His sister, meanwhile, was more interested in the people in the portrait.

"Look at the ladies' gowns!" she cried happily. "So much lace, and such lovely frilled skirts! And the gentlemen so manly in their wigs. I do so love to see a gentleman in a wig. Forgive me, Mr Merrington, but I cannot quite like the present fashion for hair with not a bit of powder to it. So informal!"

"When was this painted, would you say? Twenty or thirty years ago?" he said.

"Oh, no, no! Fifty at least, I should say. Look at the width of the ladies' gowns, and the fullness of the gentlemen's coats. Such fine embroidered fabrics — brocade, most likely. Such an elegant age!"

She sighed sentimentally, and Rowena saw Richard struggling to compose his features. Clearly he had no regrets about the lack of hair powder or wigs, and for herself she far preferred the slender high-waisted gowns of the present fashion.

Mr Childs now took the miniature away to compare it with the coat of arms shown in the Peerage.

"Definitely the Bucknells' arms," he said excitedly. "So this must be some part of the family from... fifty or so years ago, you said, my dear?"

"That is my guess, yes."

"Then after dinner, I shall examine the Peerage more closely to see if I can discern who these people might be."

The rectory repast was simple but filling, and no one felt the lack of removes or elaborate dishes. There was good wine and pleasant conversation, and what more could anyone require?

After dinner, Mr Childs settled down with the peerage to unravel the line of dukes and their many offspring, while the others took it in turns to read sermons.

"Ha! I have it," he said triumphantly. "I believe this painting shows the present duke together with his two brothers and two sisters. Their relative ages and the clothes certainly suggest it, although in so small a painting it is hard to tell. Fascinating. Quite fascinating. Thank you so much for allowing me to see this evidence of your family connection, Mrs Merrington. For I think we may now be confident that one or other of these people is a parent to your mother. There can surely be no other reason for her to have such a thing in her possession."

"Indeed, it must be so," Rowena said wonderingly. "But which one?"

"There is only one way to find out," Richard said. "We must go to Marshfields and ask the Duke of Camberley."

The Childs' intake of breath was audible, but Rowena was used to Richard's insouciance around the nobility now. A duke, completely unknown to them, to be asked about long dead family members and the possibility of an illegitimate child? Why not?

She laughed, and said nothing as he began to plan their journey to Surrey.

***

Marshfields was surprisingly modern. Richard had expected something ancient, or at least as long-established as Staineybank, with an air of permanence and well-grown trees about it, but Marshfields looked as if the builders had but that moment departed. The central square of the house, he conceded, might be older, but at each corner a vast new wing protruded, the stone as clean as if newly quarried, and the surrounding flowerbeds bore pretty little shrubs no more than a foot or two high.

Richard was beginning to enjoy his recent elevation to the fringes of the nobility. Even if his rank remained merely that of a gentleman, had he been a son or grandson, he would have held the courtesy title of Marquess of Losseter, and society accorded him the appropriate respect. The coat of arms on the carriages carried all the weight of the dukedom. So he strode confidently up the wide stone steps to the front door, and handed their cards to the butler.

"I am Mr Richard Merrington, heir to the Duke of Brinshire, travelling with my wife and her friend. I am currently investigating a family matter related to the Bucknells, and I would be most obliged if his grace would be so gracious as to spare me a few minutes of his time."

The butler bowed and ushered them into a side room, where a pair of footmen poured wine and produced platters of tiny pastries from some secret fastness. Within minutes, the butler was back, with a very pretty young lady.

"How do you do?" she said in well-modulated tones. "I am Lady Grace Skelton, the duke's daughter. He would be delighted to see you, but he is still recovering from illness so I would ask that you do not stay too long. He is in the orangery. Please follow me."

The orangery was attached by a covered walkway to one of the protruding wings of the house, so they walked through several grandiose apartments and then some more modestly appointed before Lady Grace led them into a warm, light-filled room the height of two storeys, completely filled with shrubs and trees. The long wall facing south was mostly glass, and even the roof had many skylights, to let in as much light as possible. Great flowering shrubs towered above their heads as they walked through it, filling the air with exotic perfumes.

"Look!" Rowena whispered to Richard. "Bananas! Oranges... lemons... what are those over there?"

"Pomegranates," said Lady Grace, turning her head towards them. "There are mangoes, too, on the far side. My mother's little project. Wonderful, is it not?"

"So warm!" Rowena said.

Lady Grace laughed. "Yes, even in winter, the plants have to be kept warm. We heat water to run in pipes under the floor then. It is the perfect place to watch snow falling outside. Here is my father now. No, do not get up, Papa. You know what the physician said."

The duke was skeletally thin, his face the grey of ill-health.

"I know what he said," the duke said tersely, rising with difficulty to his feet, "but there are certain courtesies a gentleman must always offer, especially to a new bride. My dear, I wish you—" He stopped with a sharp intake of breath. "But... how is this? You are the very image of my sister Caroline."

"And that," Richard said smoothly, "is the family problem which we would like to resolve. Clearly my wife is connected in some way to the Bucknells, but we cannot work out how."

Rowena produced the miniature from her reticule. "I found this among my mother's few possessions, your grace."

"Ha! I remember this portrait being painted. It was commissioned for my coming of age, and just before my sisters' entry into society. My brother was nineteen, then and Harry... ah, poor Harry! Gracie, ring the bell for Moffatt, will you? Your mother had this amongst her possessions, Mrs Merrington? It shows the five of us... myself, the heir, the Marquess of Ramsey, as I was then. Aubrey was the next in line. Then Harry, but he died when he was just seventeen. And the two girls. Caroline, as you know, married Brinshire — Losseter as he was then. And Rosalind... alas, poor Rosalind. She died young, too."

The butler came in and bowed.

"Ah, Moffatt, there you are. Send a man down to the Dower House to see if Lord Aubrey is at home, and ask if he would be good enough to attend us here. His memory is better than mine, these days, so he might have some information for you, Mrs Merrington. And Moffatt, fetch the coming of age portrait down from the attics. Ask Williamson. That man is always in the attics, so he is bound to know where it is. My secretary," he added in an undertone, when the butler had bowed and left. "Knows all the family secrets. Secretaries always do. But my manners have quite deserted me. Please, do sit down and tell me about Brinshire. How is the old rogue? In better shape than I am, I trust."

"He is very well," Richard said, holding a chair for Rowena.

"I was very sorry to hear about that boy of his," the duke said, reclaiming his own seat and shaking his head sadly. "I was fortunate in my own children. Only lost one in infancy, but Brinshire! Not a single surviving child of his own. He must be devastated."

"He bears the loss with fortitude," Richard said. "The duchess was harder hit, I believe."

"Ah, the duchess!" the duke said, his face breaking into a smile. "That took everyone by surprise, I can tell you. I met her a few times — barely more than a child, but the prettiest little thing. Goodness, how we all envied him! If my own dear duchess had not still been with me, I should have been sorely tempted to take a pretty young thing to wife myself. But there, he always had an eye for the ladies. Ha! Such a rakehell as a young man. I beg your pardon, ladies, but you are all married, so you know the type, I am sure. Brinshire... Losseter as he was then... well, he was always in trouble. Never could resist the ladies, and they could not resist him, seemingly, and not all of them had complaisant husbands. Three times I stood second for him in an affair of honour."

"Duels!" Richard said delightedly. "Oh, do tell me more, sir. I should very much like to tease him on the subject. Did he ever kill his man?"

"No, he was too skilful for that."

"A good shot, then?"

"Oh, not pistols, no. Rapiers, that was the way it was done, then. A good clean fight to first blood, and only one of his opponents was even close to his skill. The other two were on the ground in seconds. After the third time, no one challenged him again. It only guaranteed their own humiliation. He was an imposing man, Brinshire, not tall but well-built, and so light on his feet. A beautiful dancer, and a delight to watch with a sword. Heavens, the times we had! I seldom see him these days, for he is not much of a one for the political wrangling, but we were close in our youth."

The butler returned with a little train of footmen bearing refreshments, to which the ladies applied themselves with enthusiasm. Richard sipped at a glass of Madeira and listened to the duke reminiscing, for it interested him to hear something of his own duke. Growing up quite apart from the principal branch of the family, he knew very little of the man in whose footsteps he would follow, although it was hard to reconcile the somewhat irascible old man with the carefree and wild youth described by his old friend.

Eventually, the duke's brother, Lord Aubrey, arrived, to exclaim over Rowena just as the duke had done, and pore over the miniature with a fond smile.

Then more footmen appeared, carrying a much larger painting, which they propped up against a wall. It was the same people and poses as in the miniature, except that it was some ten feet high, and the faces were much more clearly delineated.

"Oh, identical twins," Rowena breathed. "How fascinating! When was it painted?"

"Fifty-three years ago," Lord Aubrey said.

"And my mother was born fifty-two years ago," Rowena said. "There can be no doubt, surely, that she was the child of one of these five, even if only a natural child."

"No, that is impossible," the duke said. "I know for a fact that I have sired no illegitimate children."

"Nor I," said Lord Aubrey, "and Harry was only twelve at the time. He was precocious, certainly, but I hardly think that precocious."

"Then it must be one of the twins," Rowena said.

The duke shook his head. "They never had the opportunity. Caroline was married practically from the schoolroom, and Rosalind died very soon after this painting was completed. She was on her way to stay with a cousin in Newcastle, but the carriage overturned and she was killed, poor girl. Barely eighteen. And before that, those girls had not a moment of freedom. They could not even take a walk in the gardens without a pair of chaperons to guard their maidenly virtue."

"Were there no others who might be responsible?" Richard said. "Your father, perhaps, or an uncle? A cousin?"

The duke and his brother both shook their heads. "Caroline and Rosalind favoured their mother in looks, so it could not have come from anyone on Father's side of the family," Lord Aubrey said.

"Then it is inexplicable," Rowena said. "Perhaps it is just a strange coincidence."

For a while they were all silent, then Lord Aubrey burst out, "I do not believe in coincidence. The family resemblance is too strong. Yet I do not know how it could have happened."

Again they fell into a frustrated silence, but Richard was tolerably sure that the mystery was not as inexplicable as it seemed.

"It is a fine painting, too fine to be kept in the attic," he said carefully.

"The artist became very famous later," Lord Aubrey said. "He was just starting his career then, but he went to Italy and did very well for himself, I understand. I hear his name mentioned everywhere. It is a fine piece of work, I must agree. I have not looked at it for years, but seeing it again now… yes, a magnificent work."

"Yet it was never hung," the duke said. "After Rosalind died, I suppose it was too painful. It was commissioned for the State Drawing Room, to hang between the portraits of our mother and father, but it went straight to the attic."

"It was completed then just before Lady Rosalind went north on her fateful journey," Richard said.

"I suppose it was," the duke said.

"It was started after we returned from town that summer," Lord Aubrey said. "The painter travelled here with us, if you remember, Camberley, and set up in the Winter Dining Room... for the light, supposedly. Mostly we sat for him separately, and he fitted each of us into the right place in the picture. It was finished in August, or maybe early September... after the shooting had started, anyway. And Rosalind went away in October."

"And Mrs Merrington's mother was born in April the following year," Richard said. "What was the painter like? Young? Charming?"

The silence was profound. It was the duke who broke it first.

"No. She died. No. It cannot be so."

"Do you *know* she died?" Richard said. "Did you see the body? Is she buried here?"

"No," Lord Aubrey said, exhaling slowly. "She was buried near where the accident was. No one went to the funeral. We were all sent away for a while, to an uncle near Bath. To distract Caroline, we were told. Poor girl, she was sunk in grief for her sister. But now that I think about it, when Rosalind went away, she was accompanied by her maid, a footman and that stuffy aunt... what was her name? Aunt Horwell. None of them ever came back. Great heavens, is it possible? But how would we ever find out?"

"The accounts," Richard said. "There would be an entry in the accounts for the funeral, or perhaps just a sum of money *'to defray expenses'*. The maid would have to be paid off, and the footman if he never returned. The accounts always tell a story."

"Gracie, ring for Moffatt, will you? Tell him we need Williamson in here with the account books from fifty-three years ago. Around the time Lady Rosalind left here."

Rowena sat silent and composed although her eyes a little wider than usual. Was she about to find the solution to her ancestry? Richard could only hope so, for an unsolved mystery could fester over the years. Better by far to have it resolved here and now, however dramatic the outcome.

The secretary arrived with a huge ledger under one arm, which he opened on a table while Lord Aubrey pored over it.

"Nothing about a funeral," he said eventually. "A sum of money for Rosalind's journey, that is all. A thousand pounds — quite a large sum, but I suppose she had no idea how much she would need. But nothing after that. Williamson, do you see anything unusual about these entries, anything that might suggest that Lady Rosalind did not die?"

The secretary slowly ran his finger down the entries, turned a page, began again, turned another page, then stopped. He flipped back several pages, then forwards.

"You see something?" Lord Aubrey said.

"A curiosity, that is all, my lord. Do you see this entry, at Christmas?"

"*'Annuity to Cousin W'*. What of it? His grace dispenses any number of annuities to indigent relations or former employees."

"Except that they usually give the full name and reason. *'To John Cartwright, retired gamekeeper, an annuity of twenty pounds a year.'* Or *'To Mrs Rupert Smith, widow, the sum of forty pounds annually.'* That sort of thing. But Cousin W is never explained. It is only ever Cousin W, four hundred a year paid quarterly, and this is the very first entry, the next quarter day after Lady Rosalind's death."

"And where was the money sent?" Richard asked eagerly.

"To an attorney in Newcastle."

"Then we may hazard a guess that the W stands for Winthrop," Richard said. "Cousin Winthrop. Lady Rosalind vanishes and Cousin W appears at roughly the same time in the far north." He smiled at Rowena. "I think, my dear, we may safely conclude that your mother's mother was Lady Rosalind Bucknell, and her father... possibly a portrait painter? Do you think?"

The secretary gave a little cry. "But then... but surely... no, it's impossible!"

The duke chuckled. "We have said that several times today, and been proved wrong. What is it, man? Do you dislike Merrington's theory?"

"No, your grace, no, but... you see... there's something you should know. If Cousin W is indeed the Lady Rosalind... oh, your grace, I don't know how to tell you this."

"Come on, man. Out with it."

"The payments to Cousin W are still going on to this day. Which means—"

"That Rosalind is still alive," the duke said. "Well, I never! What a day of surprises this is turning out to be."

12: Another Journey North

Rowena's maid, Mary, was still putting the finishing touches to her hair before dinner when Richard ambled through from his adjoining room. The duke had insisted they stay at Marshfields for a couple of nights while he considered what was best to be done about Lady Rosalind, so they found themselves in a vast suite of state rooms which would have been over-ornate even for royalty.

Richard always looked splendid in evening dress, but tonight she thought he looked especially distinguished. The neckcloth was more ornately tied, perhaps, and held with a diamond pin, and was that a new waistcoat? And his hair was fashionably disordered.

"No powder to your hair, Mr Merrington? For shame!"

He laughed. "Ugh, wigs and powder! My father always said his head itched the whole time. He was tremendously glad to leave off all that nonsense. What about you? Would you have liked to wear a sailing galleon on your head, and a skirt so wide you would need to go through doors sideways?"

"I think you know the answer to that, husband. Thank you, Mary, that will do."

When the maid had gathered up discarded garments and left, she went to sit beside Richard on the bed. "Will tonight be dreadfully formal, do you suppose? I have barely grown accustomed to Staineybank, and now here we are mingling with another duke."

"I cannot answer for the degree of formality, but there will be quite a crowd. The heir and his wife are here, Lady Grace and another daughter and their husbands, and Lord Aubrey and several of his children will be joining us. But not the duchess. She keeps to her own apartments, and we are not to distress the duke by noticing her absence. All families have their little quirks, do they not?"

He hesitated, then reached out and took her hand in his, the warmth of his touch noticeable even through her evening gloves.

"Rowena... my dear... does it unsettle you, to find out this connection? We suspected something of the sort, but not... not this! Nothing like this!"

"It does not unsettle me, but it must surely unsettle the duke and his brother to learn that their sister may still be alive after all these years. To have mourned her loss, and then to discover that she was only banished for a misdemeanour."

"A misdemeanour! A grievous sin for a gently brought up young lady. It went against everything she had been taught. She could not have expected to pay no penalty for stepping so far out of line."

She smiled sadly. "Oh, but when one falls in love... one behaves in all sorts of irrational ways. No, no! Not me! I was thinking of Georgie. She was so besotted with Henry and I confess, he was such a charmer, and yet feckless. The only good thing he ever did was to die, in my opinion, although do not tell Georgie I said so."

"What was his particular vice?"

"Drink, mostly, although he was not above borrowing from his friends and then forgetting to pay them back. He had prospects, in the person of an aunt who doted on him and had promised to leave him her money, but then he had a drop too much brandy at an inn and fell down the stairs, and the aunt is now looking favourably on a cousin. Fortunately, Georgie's uncle, who is an attorney, had tied up her modest dowry so tight that even Henry could not get his hands on it, so she survives on that."

"I do not know whether she is fortunate or otherwise to have no child," he said. "If money is in short supply, a child can be a great drain on the purse, but also a comfort to a bereaved widow."

"She was increasing, but when Henry died so suddenly, she miscarried," Rowena said. "Poor Georgie! I have always hoped that one day she would meet another man who would stir her heart — a *good* man, who would take care of her properly, but she seems to have set her face against marriage altogether. No one, it seems, can hold comparison to the sainted Henry. Well, shall we go down? It is a little early but this room is depressing my spirits dreadfully."

He chuckled. "It is overpowering, is it not? I am glad we have a canopy over the bed, or those creatures on the ceiling would give me nightmares."

"At least we shall have plenty of room," she said. "This bed is considerable larger than our entire room at Georgie's house."

"That is not necessarily an advantage," he said blandly. "I rather enjoyed having to squeeze into that narrow little bed."

"It was fun, was it not? I had to hold on to you all night to be sure not to fall out."

Laughing together and still holding hands, they made their way downstairs for dinner. The evening was just as crowded as Richard had predicted, for they sat down more than twenty at table, and the noise of the family gathering was overwhelming as everyone chatted freely to everyone else without the least formality. The talk was all of the wonder of the day, Rowena's appearance and the possibility that Lady Rosalind might still be alive. Many suggestions were made for determining the truth of the matter, from sending an army of lawyers to Northumberland to root her out wherever she might be to leaving her alone in her isolation.

It was the heir's wife, the Marchioness of Ramsey, who voiced the latter view. "She knows precisely where her family is and if she chooses not to contact us, even after so many years, then she must have her reasons, and we should respect that," she said forcefully.

"But suppose she was constrained to remain secret," the marquess said. "She was no doubt told that this annuity — four hundred pounds a year which presumably she depended on — would stop if she ever revealed her identity to a soul. She might be terrified of ending up in the workhouse in her old age."

"She must know that I would never do that to her," the duke said. "My own sister! Whatever Father may have said or done, he is gone and I am head of the family now. I could never reject her. We must find her, and bring her home. And she will want to meet her granddaughter. But how is it best to be done? The annuity is sent to an attorney, so we will start with him."

"He may not tell you," Richard said. "These legal types are very close-mouthed about their clients."

"I am a duke, so of course he will tell me," he said loftily, making everyone laugh.

Richard held up a hand. "I have a better plan, if you will hear it, your grace, which does not involve asking anyone to break a confidence. My wife's mother was baptised at St Michael's church in the diocese of Durham. She lived in a house called Holly Cottage. I propose to go to Durham and obtain a list of all the churches in the see dedicated to St Michael and visit each in turn, asking for Holly Cottage. When we find one, I shall send my wife to knock on the door. If it is the right house, she will be recognised at once."

The duke laughed. "That sounds like a good plan, Merrington, but I might send one of my own people with you, just to reassure Rosalind, if we find her, that she is welcome here if she wishes to return."

"I should like to go, if I may," the marquess said. "Charity, will you accompany me?"

"With pleasure," she said, "although I am not sure that Mrs Merrington should be jauntering about the country, not in her condition."

There was a sudden silence around the table. "Condition?" Richard said in a small voice. "But... we have only been married for three weeks and four days."

There was laughter around the table. "Quite time enough for an enthusiastic husband," one of the ladies said, making everyone laugh even more.

Rowena set down her spoon, blushing furiously. So much for that little secret.

"Rowena?" Richard said, and she could only nod.

"I do beg your pardon," the marchioness said. "Should I not have mentioned it? But once one knows the signs, it is perfectly obvious. Oh dear. I am always putting my foot in it."

"Charity, dearest," her husband said gently, "a lady prefers to make these announcements in private first, and one does not comment, even if the signs are obvious, until one is told formally. And now we will all talk about the weather until Mr and Mrs Merrington have recovered their composure."

Composure was a long time coming to Rowena, and for once she was glad when the ladies withdrew, to allow her to escape from Richard's reproachful eyes. But he was the first gentlemen to join the ladies in the drawing room, seeking her own with a broad smile on his face.

"I have been receiving a great deal of unwanted advice about my impending fatherhood," he said, with a little chuckle. "I am not going to get too excited about it just yet, since I imagine it is very early days."

"Exactly!" she said, relief washing through her. "It is far too soon to be making an announcement, even to you. Georgie guessed, of course, just as Lady Ramsey did, but—"

"How?" he said. "How did they know? Is there some sign I should have recognised? Oh — I beg your pardon. I did not mean to put you to the blush. I shall enquire no further. But should we tell the duke, do you think, when we return to Staineybank? Or should I write to him?"

"When we next see him, that will be time enough. He will be glad to know, I think, for even if this one comes to nothing, it means that I can conceive quite easily, which is promising."

"Yes. I see." He nodded thoughtfully. "You are charmingly pragmatic about these matters, my love. *'Even if this one comes to nothing...'*."

"And even if it does not, it might be a girl," she said, with a sudden spurt of laughter. "You have four sisters, after all, and I am the second generation to produce only one girl."

He pulled a face. "Then we will just have to keep trying until we produce a boy."

"So we will," she said equably. "It is what I am here for, after all."

He gave her a look she could not quite interpret, but there was no time to say more, for the instrument had been opened and she saw Lady Grace bearing down on her. She kissed him gently on the cheek, before rising to move to the pianoforte.

"How romantic!" sighed Lady Ramsey, moving in the same direction and scattering sheet music like wedding rice as she went. "I do adore seeing a newly married couple so obviously in love and happy. What will you play for us, Mrs Merrington? Oh, thank you, Grace dear. Oops! I am such a butterfingers."

Lady Grace, who had been following Lady Ramsey gathering the fallen sheets, now bent down again with a smile.

Rowena selected a piece more or less at random, discomfited by the idea that she and Richard looked like a couple in love. He had certainly spoken of love, but of her own feelings, she could not be so certain. She had confided a little in Georgie, telling her what Richard had said, but Georgie was not inclined to attach much weight to it.

"A man is always happy and fancies himself in love in the first flush of enthusiasm, but it varies with his mood, in my experience. You were making up after a quarrel, so naturally Richard was somewhat effusive, but when you next fall out, you will see the other side of the coin, and it might not be so affectionate. Do not depend on it, that is my advice."

It seemed like sound advice to Rowena. So she played and sang, and then turned the pages for Lady Grace, who was a far better performer, and pondered Georgie's words. She had had an unfortunate experience with Henry, it was true, but not everyone was so unlucky. As Lady Grace Skelton played, her husband gazed at her, a gentle smile on his lips, and no one could doubt his affection for his wife. After several years of marriage, he was still deeply in love.

Only time would tell whether Richard would turn out to be another George Skelton or a Henry Hastings.

***

With a full day at Marshfields while travel plans were made, Rowena passed the hours happily in the orangery. The building fascinated her, with its heady perfumes from exotic plants and the fruits burgeoning in the heat. The duke spent his afternoons there, gazing out of the tall windows at the gardens laid out below, while one or other of his daughters or daughters-in-law attended him and kept him entertained. He was quite happy to allow Rowena to keep him entertained, too, since she was now an unofficial member of the family.

Richard came in occasionally to see her, and once to ask if she wished to walk in the gardens, but she was content to sit with the duke in the warmth.

"I love this place," she said. "Such a pleasant, peaceful place to sit and while away the hours."

"Exactly how I feel," the duke said. "When the duchess suggested the idea of an orangery, I could not see the point, but now I spend much of my day in here."

"How lucky you are to have such a wonderful spot to sit in," she said. "I shall remember it long after I have left Marshfields."

"Then I shall fetch my sketchbook, and try to capture it for you, to help you remember," Richard said.

While Richard sketched, the duke wanted to know more about Rowena, so she told him everything she knew about her mother, and what she had been told about her grandmother.

"So you understood your grandmother was dead?"

"Yes. My mother said she was sent south to Oxford to be brought out into society, and that her mother died shortly after that. But now I am not sure what to believe. Is it possible that this *'Cousin W'* is not Lady Rosalind at all, but someone quite different? The aunt, perhaps, who accompanied her?"

"Aunt Horwell? She must be long dead. She was well past forty when she left here. Of course, it is perfectly possible that Rosalind is indeed dead, and someone else is living on that annuity, but we shall only know that when we find where it is going. Ramsey has my authority to lean on the attorney in Newcastle, if need be." He gave a rumble of laughter. "He would enjoy that, actually."

Rowena pondered that. "If Aunt Horwell is dead, and Lady Rosalind is still there, then she must be quite alone in the world. Even her original servants, who knew her as a girl, may be dead or retired by now. Imagine her, exiled to Northumberland, with no one to talk to who knows her history. How lonely she must be!"

The duke sighed. "That is the cross she chose to bear, I suppose, when she ventured off the path of righteousness."

"She has paid a heavy price for her sin," Rowena said quietly. "One moment's folly in her youth, and she was only eighteen, after all. Which of us is wise at that age? Poor lady."

"Well, if she is still there in her little cottage, surviving on four hundred a year which would not even have paid for her gowns at one time, then she must come home," he said firmly. "Heavens, if I had known, she could have come home years ago, and been happy again. Poor Rosalind. If you find her, tell her that her long exile is over at last."

***

With the addition of the Marquess and Marchioness of Ramsey to their party, travel became even more pleasurable. Rowena discovered that the deference due to the heir to a duke differed greatly between a mere mister and a marquess. She had thought the innkeepers and flunkeys excessively obsequious before, but that was as nothing compared to the reception accorded to the marquess when he swept imperiously into a hostelry, his footman rushing before him crying, "Make way for the Marquess of Ramsey! Pray attend to the Marquess of Ramsey at once!" And they did, pushing each other aside and prostrating themselves, neglecting their other guests shamefully, and repeating the footman's cries so loudly that crowds wandered in from the street to see if there were a murder going on, or a mill at the very least. It was a wonder to behold.

Charity Ramsey, however, was very much the opposite, for there was nothing in the least imperious about her. She was rather too inclined to fall out of the carriage, and one footman seemed to have the sole job of escorting her about, in order to catch her when she tripped and to pick up dropped items. She neither looked nor acted like a future duchess, and

Rowena could only be thankful that when her own time came to support her husband in his high estate, she would have at least one friend who was just as ill-suited for the rôle as she was.

The marchioness also had no reserve whatsoever, so within two miles of leaving Marshfields, they were all on Christian name terms, and before the first stage was reached, she was spilling the secrets of her marriage.

"I did not for one moment believe he was serious," she said, leaning towards Rowena. "Well, I mean, look at me — no oil painting, am I? And not duchess material, any rational person would have thought, and he could have had anyone at all. He had only to crook his little finger and they would have come running."

"They *did* come running," the marquess said, with a little smile.

"Yes, to your bed!" Charity said. "Heavens, he was such a rake when I first knew him! So how could I ever have imagined he was serious when he started making up to me? I had always thought, if I married at all, it would be some mild-mannered nobody — a clergyman, probably — attracted by my six thousand pounds and a hefty dose of pity. I never expected a future duke to hurl himself at my feet, literally, making impassioned speeches. I thought he was making a May game of me, frankly. What could he possibly see in someone like me?"

"Have you forgotten our first meeting, my love?" he said, smiling at her with such a glow in his eyes that Rowena blushed herself. "A viscountess was rather cutting to two inoffensive acquaintances, and you said she was very rude, and told me I should cut her. And I did, even though she had been a friend for a long time."

"Your mistress, you mean, and she *was* rude. A nasty, small-minded woman."

"Indeed, and yet I had never noticed it before. Much of society, I discovered when I saw it through your eyes, was nasty and small-minded. I had never encountered anyone so honest before, and it fascinated me. By our third meeting I knew I wanted to marry you. But she would not have me," he said, turning to Rowena with a rueful face. "It took me three years to persuade her to take pity on a poor lovelorn marquess."

Georgie leaned across the carriage to pat his hand sympathetically. "But you won her heart in the end, my lord. How romantic."

"I think she just realised I was not going to give up," he said, with a quick laugh. "And I had thoroughly reformed by then. I would not go quite so far as to say I became a serious and useful member of society, and may never reach that point, but I gave up all the gaming and drunken wildness, and I never looked at another woman after I met Charity. She made me wait a long time, but she is a woman in a million, well worth waiting for."

Georgie sighed sentimentally, but Charity said, "And now that you know all about us, you must tell us your own story, Rowena, for it took you considerably less time to reach an understanding than we did."

"Indeed," Rowena said drily. "We met on a Friday, Richard proposed on the following Monday, I accepted on Tuesday, and we were married by special licence on the Saturday. That is... let me see, eight days."

Charity's eyes were huge. "Oh, how charming! Love at first sight!"

They both laughed at that.

"Not quite," Richard said. "My cousin the duke insisted I marry as soon as possible, and threw three daughters of an earl at my head, all of them vapid and insipid and unendurable. Rowena was a hundred times more sensible so naturally I proposed at once."

"And since I was a penniless orphan trying unsuccessfully to obtain a post as a governess, naturally I accepted," she said.

"Oh but..." Charity said, her gaze switching from one to the other. "You seem... so happy."

"Happiness is not only to be found in a love match," Rowena said calmly, reaching for Richard's hand and giving it a reassuring squeeze. "Even a match as practical as ours may bring a great deal of happiness, where there is respect and consideration and gratitude... and enough food to eat for the rest of one's life."

Charity smiled, but Rowena thought it rather a sad smile, as if she pitied them. "Gratitude? Is that enough?"

"Gratitude is a good start," she said. "It is the tiny bud of an unopened flower, which with sunshine and warmth will unfurl its petals into affection and eventually the full bloom of true love. God willing, Richard and I have our whole lives to grow to love each other. There will be shared joys and no doubt sorrows too, but whatever comes, we will weather the storms together."

Georgie sighed again, but this time she was the one who looked sad. No doubt she was remembering the storms in her own short-lived marriage, but whether more years would have brought Henry to respectable gentility or ruination was open to debate. Rowena glanced complacently at Richard, who would never, she was certain, fall down the stairs in a drunken stupor.

Charity may think little of gratitude, but Rowena thanked God every night for her good fortune. If Richard had never made his impulsive offer, she would have left Staineybank that day for a desolate and miserable existence, she would never have had a child growing inside her or a comfortable home waiting for her.

As for Richard himself — the bud of gratitude was already beginning to open its petals into something more. Every day she admired and respected him a little more, and took another cautious step on the road to affection. And from there, could love be far behind?

13: Holly Cottage

Richard knew he should be pleased with life. He had a lovely and amiable wife, there was a child to look forward to and he no longer needed to watch the pennies. And yet... something inside him yearned for more.

He recalled Rowena saying that her place was beside him, and despite her protestations, he could not avoid the feeling that she saw it as no more than her wifely duty. When the marchioness had spoken of love, Rowena had talked of flower buds opening in time, and of storms to be weathered. When he had talked of having a son, she had said, *'That is what I am here for'.* And that was true, but he wanted so much more from his marriage.

Was that wrong of him? Should he be satisfied with a complaisant wife who would do her duty meekly, but offer no more than that?

On their slow progress north, he found himself brooding more and more on the question. He watched Rowena whenever her attention was elsewhere, trying to glean hints from her manner or words of which way her mind was working. Was the flower bud beginning to open up, or was he wishing for the moon? If only he could be content!

When they reached Durham and had secured rooms at the Queen's Head, they all went directly to the cathedral precincts to obtain information about the parishes in the diocese dedicated to St Michael. There were only three, which cheered them immensely. Only three towns to visit would make the task of finding Holly Cottage and Lady Rosalind Bucknell a great deal easier.

The others wished to visit friends of the marchioness who lived there, but Richard was not minded to be sociable so instead he collected his sketchbook and spent an hour or two walking around the cathedral, drawing a little and thinking of Rowena.

When he returned to the inn, he was surprised to find her sitting quietly in their parlour with her needlework.

"You did not wish to call upon these friends of Charity's?" he said.

Smiling, she shook her head. "Charity is a lovely lady, but I find her rather wearing. Have you been anywhere interesting?"

"The cathedral."

"May I see?"

He hesitated only momentarily, before opening the sketchbook to show her.

"Oh, these are beautiful! How clever you are to draw so well. May I see your drawings of the orangery?"

He watched as she leafed through the book, enjoying her pleasure in seeing the orangery again, and waiting for the moment when she turned the page.

"Oh! Is this of me? It is! I did not know you were taking my likeness as well." She looked through the rest of the book, then handed it back to him. "No other people? Just buildings?"

"I find buildings fascinating," he said, leaving hanging in the air the question of whether he found her fascinating, too.

She gazed at him, those beautiful grey eyes thoughtful. Then, taking a deep breath, as if summoning up her courage, she went on, "You have been very subdued lately, Richard. Is this endless travelling wearing you down or is there more to it?" Hastily she added, "You need not tell me anything if you had rather not, of course, for I have no wish to pry, but I am your wife, after all. If anything troubles you, you may always confide in me. If you wish to, I mean."

He was silent, pondering how much to tell her. To give himself time, he walked across the room and poured himself a glass of wine. A sip, and then a second one. So tempting, to spill his heart's desires to her! But he had already spoken of love to her… dared he mention it again?

He pulled a chair nearer to her and sat down, twirling the glass absently in his hands. She was watching him, her colour a little heightened, but waiting patiently for him to sort out his thoughts.

"It is what you said to Charity," he burst out eventually. "About gratitude. I am not sure I want your gratitude, Rowena. No… that came out wrong. Let me say very clearly that I am happy to call you wife, whatever the terms. I was… I *am* myself grateful you agreed to marry me and saved me from the torture of fending off scores of bird-witted daughters of the nobility, but what I feel for you is so much more than gratitude. Am I wrong to hope that you will come to feel more than gratitude, too?"

She smiled, then, looking relieved. "Is that what this is about? Oh, Richard! Let me explain it to you, for you cannot possibly understand. No one who lives on his own estate with an income of twelve hundred pounds a year can possibly know anything of poverty. When my father was alive, we had enough to live upon, with care. He was rector, so he had the greater and lesser tithes, but it was a poor parish, not worth more than two hundred a year, at best, and often a lot less. We had two servants but I did most of the cooking and sewing. Meat on the table was a treat, and if I needed a new gown or half-boots, then we had to buy fewer candles, or make the worn out cooking pot last another year. When he died, by the time the little bequests to the servants and the sexton and verger and the poor of the village were made, I was left with forty seven pounds three shillings and seven pence."

He nodded, beginning to see her point.

"When I went to my uncle, well, he was a genial man but he never thought to make me an allowance. Once I mentioned not having anything suitable to wear for an evening engagement, and he gave me fifty pounds — fifty! I had never had so much to spend on myself before. That lasted me for a long time. But when he died, my cousin never gave me anything at all. He expected his wife to clothe me, but of course she never did. And although there was plenty of food on the table, I ate with the children in the schoolroom more often than not."

"Even though you were family?"

"Oh yes. If there were guests for dinner, I was expected to join them in a borrowed gown so that Maria could portray herself as benevolently caring for the poor relation, but it was all a myth. By the time I left there, I only had some fifteen pounds left to my name, but even a life as a governess seemed preferable. And then... a miracle happened. A stranger appeared with a carriage to whisk me away to the home of a duke, and even gave me a hundred pounds. And then you came along and offered me a comfortable home for the rest of my life. Can you blame me for being dazzled by it? More food than I could eat in a week at every meal. A beautiful house, an army of servants, miles of gardens to walk in, silk gowns to wear. And the little things... the cup of chocolate in bed each morning, the smooth sheets, wax candles everywhere. Everything I do, everywhere I go there are luxuries that I never, ever expected to enjoy, and my day is entirely consumed in gratitude. Simply sitting in the carriage listening to Charity, I am aware of the comfort of the squabs, my lovely velvet pelisse, the feathers in my hat. Oh, the extravagance of feathers in one's bonnet! Such joy in the smallest thing."

He laughed. "Yes, I can see that, and I am delighted that such small things bring you pleasure."

"Yes, but do you see? There is so much that brings me pleasure and I am so deeply grateful for all of it. Everywhere I turn, I am surrounded by the miracle of having enough of everything — more than enough! Can you blame me for being dazzled by the sheer wonder of a life of plenty? To me it is so astonishing that my head is filled with awe at my good fortune. And you are not the least of it, husband, dear."

That cheered him a little. "Even though I am not a great, bruising fellow like Ramsey?"

"Especially that. A great, bruising fellow would be rather intimidating, I should think. Whereas you are the kindest, most generous man in Christendom, and, at the risk of becoming boringly repetitive, I must tell you that I am deeply grateful for it."

That made him laugh again, but he was still bemused. "I understand that you are thankful for your new life, but—"

"You want more than gratitude... I know. And one day, all this will be normal to me. I will grow accustomed to this amazing abundance, where even travel is easy, with private parlours and wine always available and the best muslin under my fingers." With a sigh, she ran a hand over her skirts. "And then, when I am less blinded by astonishment, I will be able to see you clearly as a man, and not just as a benevolent provider of luxuries. That is when I shall, I hope, be able to love you as you want and as you deserve."

"Ah," he said. It was not quite what he had hoped for but it was promising for the future. Then he laughed again. "I must sound like the most ungrateful man alive, pushing you to say what you do not yet feel. Forgive me, my love."

She blushed. "There is nothing to forgive. Oh! I hear Charity's voice in the yard outside. They are back, then. We still have an hour before dinner. Shall we slip away to our room for a rest?"

"A rest?"

"Or whatever more interesting occupation occurs to us."

With a chuckle, he set down his glass and held out his hand to her. "What an excellent suggestion, wife."

***

The first church of St Michael turned out to be in a tiny village not far from the coast, comprising little more than a straggle of fishermen's cottages. Rowena had been hopeful, but there was no inn and no Holly Cottage, and so, reluctantly, they accepted defeat.

"The next nearest church is at Alnwick," Richard said dubiously, "but that is a great deal larger than a village."

"But the only other one is at Berwick-upon-Tweed, which is even larger," Lord Ramsey said. "Besides, Alnwick is nearer, and it has a White Swan inn, according to the guides, which is promising. Let us try it, anyway."

The inn was easily found, and having secured accommodation, the marquess said to the innkeeper, "We are looking for a house called Holly Cottage. Do you know it?"

"Aye, sir, yer lordship, sir. Tis just a short step beyond the market square. Mr and Mrs Homewood live there."

Rowena's spirits soared and almost instantly plummeted again. After all their efforts to find Holly Cottage, to discover that Lady Rosalind was no longer there was a dreadful blow.

"It is no use," she murmured to Richard. "She is dead... or moved away, perhaps. It is a long time since my mother left her home, so why we should expect to find everything just as she said, I cannot imagine."

"We will go there anyway," Richard said equably. "They may know something of her present whereabouts, and remember, the annuity is still being paid to someone."

Holly Cottage was larger than Rowena had expected. Her mother had described it minutely, but it seemed that since her day, the modest double-fronted dwelling had been extended by a new wing to one side, somewhat larger than the original house. Behind it was another new building, a stable and coach house. But there was still a holly tree by the gate, and the orchard at the side of the house still sported a swing, where three children were playing under the watchful eye of a young woman and a maid.

"Children," Rowena said, smiling. "How lovely!"

Richard tucked her arm in his. "One day we will sit and watch our children play like that."

A sudden rush of affection swept over Rowena, taking her by surprise. Their children! What a joy that would be, to see them grow and change and become people with their own quirks and funny little ways. They would be a family, mother and father and however many children God saw fit to bestow on them, and he wanted that as much as she did. At that moment, when they were in perfect accord, she did not doubt that she loved Richard completely and utterly.

Tears rose to her eyes, but she blinked them back. There would be time enough for sentiment later, but now the young woman had seen them and was walking towards the gate where they clustered.

"Good day!" she called out to them as she approached. "May I help you in any way?"

Rowena was still too unsettled to speak, and Richard seemed equally unsure. The marquess, however, was not a man to hold back.

"I am the Marquess of Ramsey and I am here looking for my aunt, the Lady Rosalind Bucknell," he said, pulling out a card and handing it to her.

She bobbed him a nervous curtsy. "But there is no one here by that name. I do not know her... my lord."

"Winthrop," Richard muttered. Then, more loudly, "Her name was Winthrop, Ramsey."

"Ah, so it was. I beg your pardon, madam. Do you know of a Mrs Winthrop?"

Her eyes narrowed, as her gaze flicked from Lord Ramsey to Richard and back again. "I... I will ask. Sir. My lord."

With another bob, she walked briskly back to the children, who were watching interestedly, the youngest carried by the maid. She said something to the maid, then they all trooped indoors by a side door.

"That went well," Georgie said with a quick laugh.

"The name Winthrop means something to her, anyway," Richard said.

"But whatever she calls herself, she is not here," Rowena said sadly, all the excitement leaching out of her. "Homewood, that is the name of the family who live here."

"They might know where she has gone," he said. "Courage! We will find out what has happened to her."

He smiled at her so warmly that she was cheered again. How could she be downhearted when Richard was here with her, and entirely on her side? Had anyone ever been on her side before, apart from her parents and Georgie? From everyone else, she had seen only the casual indifference of distant relations, at best.

For several minutes they stood meekly beside the gate awaiting the return of the young lady, and no doubt a polite dismissal. When she came, however, she was accompanied by a stylishly dressed woman of around seventy, who was holding Lord Ramsey's card. Was it...? No, surely it could not be...? But the age was right, and those eyes! Her own grey eyes gazing at the group with a smile on her face.

"Ramsey?" she said, picking him out at once. "Is it you? William's boy, I take it?"

"He is Camberley now, of course. Then you must be... Aunt Rosalind?"

She laughed merrily. "Heavens, I have not used that name for an age. Come inside, do, and bring your friends." Her gaze swept over them all, past Rowena, then abruptly back again with a little gasp. "Oh, but... my dear, who *are* you? A sister of Ramsey's? Or are you one of Caroline's?"

"Neither," Rowena said, laughing. "I am one of yours. I am Mrs Richard Merrington now, but I was Rowena Holt, daughter of Jenny."

There was an astonished screech, then the gate was flung open and Rowena found herself wrapped in the scented embrace of the Lady Rosalind Bucknell. Her grandmother.

Somehow, though they were both crying, they were got back through the gate and up the short path to the front door, and inside, although neither would let go of the other.

Crowding into the hall, Rowena was aware of an elderly man watching them.

"Ben, Ben, it is Jenny's daughter! Jenny has a *daughter!* Look! Is it not astonishing? Can you see the likeness? Ben is my husband now, Rowena, but he is also Jenny's father and your grandfather."

"The painter?" she cried. "You came back from Italy?"

"Many years ago," he said, his eyes crinkling at the edges as he smiled. "I could not stay away from my beloved Rose forever. We have been married for more than thirty years now. But I thought Jenny had no children? How old are you, child?"

"Three and twenty, sir."

"There you are then, my dear. Jenny must have been..." He paused, calculating in his head. "Thirty when you were born? Nine and twenty? Something of the sort."

"But why did she not tell me?" Lady Rosalind wailed. "How is she, my dear Jenny?"

Rowena froze. She did not know! "My mother... I am so sorry, she is dead. She died almost ten years ago."

"Ohhh! My poor Jenny! But let us not stand upon ceremony. Come into the drawing room. Thomas! Where are you? Ah, there you are. The best claret for our guests — no, champagne! We must have champagne, and ask Lucy to send up some cakes or whatever she has. Come in, come in, all of you."

Thoroughly bemused, Rowena allowed herself to be shepherded through the unpretentious older part of the house into the new wing, where the rooms were much more ornate. The drawing room was adorned with some splendid paintings, and a magnificent pianoforte and a harp occupied one end of it.

Everyone seemed to be talking at once, but amidst all the chatter, Rowena understood only one thing clearly — that she had a complete *family* now. As well as her husband and the prospect of children of her own, she had grandparents, and an uncle and two aunts, it transpired, and several cousins. Word had been sent out, and the room gradually filled with excited relations, exclaiming over her likeness to Lady Rosalind, hugging and kissing her, chattering away until her head hurt.

Yet it was too bewildering. She could not make her befuddled brain understand it. For years she had supposed that her grandmother was dead, and even after Marshfields and the hope that perhaps she was still alive after all, she had imagined a sad and lonely old lady. Now she was confronted with a woman who had sent her illegitimate daughter away as soon as she was old enough to be married off, and had promptly begun a new life, surrounding herself with a new, legitimate family.

Rowena knew she should be pleased she had found happiness at last, but all she felt was resentment. This large, lively family was hers, too... it *should* have been hers, and her mother's. If they had stayed here, surrounded by the obvious affluence now prevailing, there would never have been the struggle to survive in the rectory, or the humiliating interlude as the poor relation with her father's unwelcoming kin, or the desperate search for a position as a governess.

So when Lady Rosalind turned to her, and made some laughing remark about Rowena coming home, she could not bear it.

"But it is not my home, is it?" she said, so loudly that the chatter died away. "It has never been my home, because you sent my mother away. We struggled just to feed and clothe ourselves, while you lived in luxury. Why? Why did you do that? Were you so ashamed of her that you could not wait to be rid of her? If I had not had the good fortune to meet my husband, and it was the merest chance, for our paths would never normally have crossed, I should have been earning my living as a governess by now, and I would never have known how little you cared about my mother."

14: Home

Somehow they got her out of the room and into a smaller parlour, her grandmother and grandfather, and Richard went too, because Rowena was clinging desperately to his arm, the one safe island in the turbulent sea of her emotions. She was crying, she found. Her grandfather proffered a handkerchief, and then silently pushed a glass of something into her hand.

"Oh, my dear!" her grandmother said, sitting beside her on an overstuffed sofa. "What must you think of us! But it was the only way to keep her safe."

"Safe from what?"

"From my father," she said briskly. "He was... well, very much typical of his class, I suppose. As soon as my sister and I were old enough, he arranged marriages for us. That is what fathers did in those days. Caroline was happy with her match — Losseter was head over ears in love with her, and she was half way there in return, but I... I was not so content with the man chosen for me. And then I met Ben and knew it would not do at all. I could not possibly marry anyone else. Nor would my father ever agree to me marrying Ben, for he was merely a penniless young man with a talent with a brush in those days. If we had done nothing, I would have been married off and that would have been the end of it. So... we devised a plan. I would get myself with child, which would sink any prospect of a respectable match, and then we could bide our time. Try the brandy, my dear. I am persuaded it will do you a great deal of good."

Obediently, Rowena sipped, as her grandmother accepted a glass herself and continued her tale.

"It was a risk, of course, for he might have packed me off to an asylum, which would have been a more difficult problem to deal with, but in the end he settled for exile. He made us swear — both of us, on the Bible, if you please, since he did not trust us an inch — that we would not contact each other. If we did, then I would be in the asylum, the child would go to an orphanage and Ben would never find work again. He wanted us both to change our names, but Ben refused that. He already had a reputation, and he had no wish to begin again. So he was sent to Italy."

"Which was the making of me, actually," he said with a smile. "I was in great demand amongst the English living there who wanted miniatures to send home, and that led to work from the locals, too. I made my fortune very swiftly."

"But he stayed in Italy for some years, waiting. Harry was our conduit for letters for a while, and then an old school friend, for we dared not write directly. Eventually, Ben became famous enough that even a duke could not destroy him. But for me, and for Jenny, the threat of the asylum and orphanage hung over us the whole time. There was only one way to put ourselves beyond my father's reach, and that was to marry. A husband would have the only power over his wife, and even a duke could not prevail against that right. My husband was waiting for me in Italy, but Jenny's case was more difficult."

She sighed, shaking her head sadly. "You asked why I sent her away, my dear. The answer is that no husband could be found for her here. Aunt Horwell was my watchdog, who no doubt reported my every move to my father and certainly took the greatest pleasure in broadcasting my shame to everyone in Alnwick. The whole town shunned me as a fallen woman, and shunned Jenny as a bastard. So as soon as she was sixteen, I sent her to an old friend in Oxford to be found a husband as soon as may be. Jenny knew the reasons for it, and she married within a twelvemonth. It was not a great match, but respectable, I thought — a clergyman. Yet you were in poverty? I am sorry for it. I wish she had let me know, but we had agreed — no letters. It was safer that way, and perhaps she did not like to ask for charity. Certainly I would have helped. I... we... were no longer in need. Ben came here as soon as we saw the notice of Jenny's marriage in the *Gazette.* All need for secrecy was gone then, so he courted me in form, and we were married within six months. His money paid for the improvements to the house, and my respectable married state brought a change in the town. Our society was sought, we have friends now and we have been happy, have we not, my love?"

"Indeed we have."

He smiled fondly at his wife, one hand resting on her shoulder, and they exchanged a glance of such pure love that Rowena was smitten with envy. Oh, to have such a perfect understanding, to live in blissful harmony with one's beloved! She turned her gaze on Richard, and to her astonishment, she saw him watching her with the same look on his face — the little smile, the shining eyes, the glow of affection... of love.

She could not resist smiling back. How wonderful it was to be loved by such a good, honourable man! She was very blessed.

***

Richard, Rowena and Georgie stayed only one night in Alnwick, for Rowena wanted to be gone. She said little, but her mouth was set in a firm line, and no persuasions from the Homewoods changed her mind. She had met her grandmother, and now she would go home to Staineybank.

The Ramseys wanted to stay for a few days, so they moved into a spacious guest apartment at Holly Cottage, and only the two Brinshire carriages set off for the south.

Richard watched Rowena carefully on the journey home, but she gave no outward sign of distress. To any enquiry, from Georgie or himself, she replied that she was perfectly well, but would be glad to be at home again. She ate with her usual enthusiasm and slept well, so he had no reason for concern, but he worried about her anyway.

They spent the Sabbath at Leeds, attending divine service in a magnificent church and walking around the wide, well-paved streets admiring the many fine buildings and signs of enterprise and prosperity in the town. Georgie fell in with a party of travellers from Oxford who wanted to visit the Literary Hall, but Rowena was tiring, so Richard took her back to the hotel and ordered a cold collation. She ate a little, then sat in a window seat overlooking the street, still bustling with people attending a later service or visiting friends.

Richard picked up a book at random, but he could not concentrate enough to read, so eventually he simply sat, gazing at his wife's profile.

After a while, she turned to him with a slight smile. "You must not worry about me, you know."

He was thrilled that she raised the subject herself. "Must I not? But how can I help it when you are not your usual self. Are you unhappy?"

"No, not at all," she said, sounding surprised. "What makes you think so?"

"I merely wondered, after all that we found at Alnwick. You were upset at the time."

"Upset… yes, but not unhappy. Simply… disappointed, I suppose. But I suppose it is always so, is it not? One anticipates a glorious reunion and then… it is not so." She rose and walked across to sit beside him where he sprawled in a chair, wine glass resting on the table. "How could she do it, Richard? How could she send her daughter away and then never see her again, never write to her, never go to see her? She must have known where my mother was but it was as if she had never existed. She had her new life, her husband, three new children, and the sixteen years with her first daughter were utterly forgotten."

"Not forgotten, I imagine. How could anyone forget a child?"

"Exactly!" she cried. "No one could, yet she never once tried to make contact with her. Even when her father died, and she was free from any threat, she did nothing. I cannot understand it."

"Nor I," he said, frowning. It was an aspect of the affair that had not previously occurred to him. "It is almost as if she was ashamed of her. People are very censorious about illegitimacy, after all."

"She might have been ashamed of her own behaviour," Rowena said. "That I can understand. She was a duke's daughter, after all, and she threw that away for entirely selfish reasons. But that was not my mother's fault! No child, legitimate or otherwise, asks to be born. My grandmother might have regretted her own actions, but she had no business to cast the shadow of her own wrongdoing on her innocent daughter."

He could not quarrel with her argument. "Selfish..." he murmured. "Yes, she has been very selfish. She refused the no doubt prestigious match arranged by her father in favour of a penniless artist. Even today the daughter of a nobleman is expected to marry sensibly, but in those days such wilfulness must have been scandalous indeed. No wonder her father pretended she was dead. As far as he was concerned, she *was* dead, or as good as. And then as soon as she could, she disposed of the illegitimate daughter and contracted a respectable marriage to her lover, which gave her standing in local society, and seemingly never gave a thought to the daughter cast aside. Yes, she has been utterly selfish."

"Whereas you..." Rowena began.

"I?"

"The duke wanted you to marry at once, and you did. Admittedly, I was not the most sensible choice but—"

"You were the *perfect* choice," he said firmly.

She blushed a little, lowering her eyes. "Be that as it may, you made no complaint. You simply got on with it, and did your duty. Georgie says you are easy-going, and she is right. You never make a fuss about anything. Unlike me! I made the most enormous fuss at St Jude's and you have never once berated me for it. No, no!" She held up one hand to forestall his protestations. "Do not deny it. I acted very badly."

He reached for her hand and gently kissed her fingers. "It was most unlike you, for you are the most even-tempered lady I have ever met."

"Georgie thinks it is because I am increasing," she said, with a little blush. "It makes one emotional, seemingly."

“Ah, that makes sense,” he said, keeping a light hold of her hand and hoping she would not notice. “The business at Holly Cottage was upsetting, too, but you seem to have recovered well from that.”

She smiled then with such warmth that a bolt of pure happiness shot through him.

“Ah, yes, but you see I have discovered an antidote to all the little bumps in the road of life. I have realised that even in the darkest moments, I have my personal physician who provides me with the perfect tonic — and no need for bloodletting or purges, either.”

"Oh.” He had no idea what to make of that — a physician? Had she taken medical advice without him knowing?

She gave a little laugh and squeezed his hand. “Richard... surely you can understand me? I *was* upset at Holly Cottage, and perhaps I would have exploded again, but then you smiled at me and I realised that my grandmother’s action need not distress me, not when I have you by my side.”

“Oh,” he said again, surprised but inordinately pleased. “I shall be sure to smile at you very often, in that case.”

“Please do, as often as you like.” Another little blush. “Every time you smile at me in that way... oh, I cannot even describe it! But it warms me to my very heart, and I know that my life is incomparably better now that you are a part of it.”

“Oh!” He shook his head, bemused. “Listen to me! I sound like an idiot, but you leave me without words. If this is your idea of gratitude, then I like it very much.”

“Is it just gratitude? Or something else? I cannot tell. I am all at sea just now. So much has happened in a very short time, so that I hardly know where I am, still less what I feel. All I know is that you make me very happy.”

He kissed her hand again, first the fingers, and then the palm, before pressing it to his cheek, eyes close. "And I too," he said with a sigh. "Do you think perhaps... maybe... is it possible that what you feel is... well, something like love?"

"I think it might be," she whispered.

"Oh," he said, for the fourth time, opening his eyes again. And there she was, her face just inches from his, smiling at him with such affection that he was quite overwhelmed. With a little cry of joy, he gathered her into his arms and lifted her onto his lap. There they stayed, quite content, unspeaking, until Georgie returned and sent them off, still delirious with joy, to dress for dinner.

***

Staineybank slumbered under cloudy August skies, the air humid and heavy, the tired trees already showing hints of the autumn to come. The duke and duchess themselves emerged to welcome them home, together with Cousin Hester, Mr Hammond and Mr Godley, and all five of the Merrington ladies. His mother, Richard noticed with amusement, took it upon herself to direct the servants unloading the luggage, oblivious of Cousin Hester or the butler. All his sisters wore new, fashionable gowns, and his mother bore a showy new brooch on her fichu. He would have to find out the cost of that later.

"Well, well, well, here you are at last!" the duke cried, giving Rowena a kiss on each cheek. "Let me look at you. Are you well, my dear?"

"I am very well, your grace. Very well indeed," she murmured, with that slight blush that Richard had come to love so well.

"Excellent," he said, briskly. "But come inside, do, for there is rain coming any minute, I am sure of it. There now, Lily will take care of you. Richard, come through to my study. You must be parched, travelling in August. Such thirsty work."

Meekly, Richard left Rowena to the ladies and followed the duke through the formal apartments to the study, accepting the brandy that was pushed into his hand without demur.

"Is she indeed well?" was the duke's first question. "After all that has happened—"

"She is perfectly well, Duke. So well, in fact, that you may have an heir by the spring."

"Ah!" he said, with a smile of satisfaction. "Well done, boy, well done! And if it is a girl, of course, that will be welcome, too. There is plenty of time, after all. You are still young, you have years to get yourself an heir. So tell me all about this sister of Caroline's. Alive all these years and hiding away in the north! Whoever would have guessed it? All families have their little secrets, but that is more surprising than most. The Bucknells are such a restrained family, as a rule. Not Ramsey, though! He was very rackety in his youth, but the older generation were very staid, or so one would have said."

"I suppose there is one in every family who breaks away from the herd," Richard said thoughtfully.

"A black sheep? True enough, although it is usually the men who run wild, not the women. What is she like now? For that is what my Caroline would have looked like, had she lived."

They talked for some time of the inhabitants of Holly Cottage, and of the Bucknells generally, as the duke gradually depleted the brandy decanter.

Richard drank more abstemiously, for with the expense of a decent brandy, he had rarely indulged. But that put him in mind of another matter.

"My mother and sisters are looking very well dressed these days, and I know to the penny what their pin money will allow. I hope they have not been wheedling money out of you, sir, for if once you start, there will be no end to it."

The duke laughed. "Now, now, you must not object if I spoil them a little, for they brighten my life so much. They keep Lily contented here, for one thing. If not for your sisters, she would have been off to Cheshire long since. And your mother has been so helpful to Hester, relieving her of some of the burden of keeping this place on an even keel, so when she mentioned that none of them had gowns fit to grace a duke's table... what can I do? It pleases me to see them happy and if a few new gowns are the price to be paid, how can I possibly object?"

"You must be careful, sir, or they will fill the entire house with new gowns if you let them. I gave them an allowance and never let them wheedle me out of a penny more."

"Hmm, they are very good at wheedling, I suspect," the duke said thoughtfully. "Very well, then, an allowance it is, and Pyott will see that they keep to it. Which reminds me... you were right about Pyott."

"Was I?" Richard said, frowning, struggling to recall what had been said about the comptroller.

"You were. You felt there was something amiss, and so it transpires. His wife's mother was left a widow about three years ago, and very poorly provided for. He had no room for her at his own cottage, for they have five little ones now, nor could he afford to support her directly, so he has been diverting small amounts from my funds. Always intending to pay it back eventually, of course. He had been supplementing his income at the card table, and when he had a good night, he replaced some of the loss. A sad case — confessed and wept all over me when I mentioned the subject, not thinking for a moment that there was any truth in it."

"That would be why I could not see it clearly," Richard said. "Sometimes money was going out, but sometimes it went in again. It made the picture hard to discern."

"Yet you knew there was something out of line," the duke said.

"It was no more than a feeling."

"Hmpf. Your feelings appear to be rather accurate. I should like you to have a look at Monk, if you will."

"Monk?"

"The bailiff. You will need to follow him around to get to know the estate. There is another fellow looks after the Gloucestershire and Welsh properties, and one for Dorsetshire... and I think he sees to Hampshire, too, but there is not much there. A footling little house and a few cottages. Hardly worth the bother, really, but Caroline and I had our wedding month there, so I keep it from sentiment. You may want to sell it after I am gone. Where was I? Oh yes, Monk. Let him show you about, but keep an eye on him, and let me know if you have any feelings on the matter. And there is a lease my attorney has been pestering me to sign, but I should like you to look it over first."

"Very well, sir. I am entirely at your disposal."

The duke grunted. "Entirely at my disposal, so long as it is something you want to do, eh? I have not forgotten that you insisted on choosing your own bride. Not that I blame you for *that.* Those Harper girls would never have done. No, you have found a much better match, although... did you discover any more about how she came to be here?"

"It is all as she told us when she arrived here — the letter from Mr Goodenough, the carriage on the appointed day, everything arranged."

"Yet there is no attorney by that name in Brinchester. Indeed, there is no one at all by that name, attorney or not. Hammond asked at the post office."

"It is a mystery," Richard said lightly, not terribly worried by it.

"Hmpf. I dare say we shall never know the reason. Well, I hope your lady mother has arranged a good dinner for us tonight. I must tell Froggett to bring up something decent from the cellar. A celebration is in order, do you not agree? Not that we should count our chickens, for no one knows better than I that these matters do not always run smoothly, but still... you have done well, my boy, you and that lady wife of yours. Very well indeed. It bodes well for the future. And you are... contented with her?"

"I am excessively contented, sir."

"Good, good. We must think about a wedding present for her — something special. Diamonds, perhaps. Or sapphires."

"What would you say to an orangery?"

***

Nothing was said at dinner to put Rowena to the blush, but the duke treated her with a gentleness that left her in no doubt that Richard had told him explicitly of her condition. The duke tucked her arm in his as soon as she arrived in the drawing room, and kept her beside him throughout dinner, banishing Richard to the other end of the table, where he sat uncomfortably in a cluster of his sisters.

When the ladies withdrew, she was relieved to escape the duke's solicitude and retreat to a sofa set in a bay window. Georgie sat with her for a while, but finding Rowena unresponsive to her conversational overtures, she was soon drawn away to the chattier group across the room, where Lily and her sister formed the centre of a laughing, teasing cluster of Merrington sisters. Mrs Merrington sat placidly with Cousin Hester, each with their embroidery.

This was what her life would be like from now on, Rowena realised. There would be no mischievous children to drag into some semblance of civilisation, no banishment to the nursery floor, no terror of being turned off without a reference. Nor would she be obliged to accept any man who deigned to offer for her simply to avoid destitution — a clergyman, most likely, with the wearying round of parish duties, and the constant struggle to pay the butcher's bill and buy shoes for a growing number of children.

She had a place in the world, at last, a place that could never be taken from her. She would have children, she hoped, and no shortage of shoes for them. She had friends — Georgie, of course, but also the Merrington ladies and the duke and his family.

Most of all, she had Richard. Her heart sped up a little as she thought of him, so kind, so understanding, so loving. She was the luckiest creature alive.

When he came through, the first of the men to emerge from the dining room, she smiled at him and patted the space beside her on the sofa. With an answering smile, he came straight to her side.

"Not talking to the ladies?" he said, taking hold of her hand, so that warmth flooded through her.

"I preferred to contemplate my good fortune. It is lovely to be home, is it not?"

His smile widened. "Indeed it is, and it is truly beginning to feel like home. But that is all due to you, my darling wife. You make Staineybank home, for me." He gave her hand a little squeeze. "Dearest, I have no idea how it was that you were brought here or who Mr Goodenough might be, but I am eternally thankful for his actions."

She lifted his hand to her lips and gently kissed it.

"As am I, my love. As am I."

With a sigh of contentment, she laid her head on his shoulder.

THE END

The next book in the series is *The Duke's Architect,* which features an orangery, a struggling architect and a lady who loves to dance. You can read a sneak preview after the acknowledgements.

For more information, go to my website at https://marykingswood.co.uk

Thanks for reading!

If you have enjoyed reading this book, please consider writing a short review on Amazon. You can find out the latest news and sign up for the mailing list at my website at https://marykingswood.co.uk.

A note on historical accuracy: I have endeavoured to stay true to the spirit of Regency times, and have avoided taking too many liberties or imposing modern sensibilities on my characters. The book is not one of historical record, but I've tried to make it reasonably accurate. However, I'm not perfect! If you spot a historical error, I'd very much appreciate knowing about it so that I can correct it and learn from it. Thank you!

About the series:

Book 0: The Duke's Heir *(a novella prequel)*

Book 1: The Duke's Architect

Book 2: The Duke's Portraitist

Book 3: The Duke's Gardener

Book 4: The Duke's Steward

Book 5: The Duke's Librarian

Book 6: The Duke's Enemy

Any questions about the series? Email me at mary@marykingswood.co.uk - I'd love to hear from you!

About the author

I write traditional Regency romances under the pen name Mary Kingswood, and epic fantasy as Pauline M Ross. I live in the beautiful Highlands of Scotland with my husband. I like chocolate, whisky, my Kindle, massed pipe bands, long leisurely lunches, chocolate, going places in my campervan, eating pizza in Italy, summer nights that never get dark, wood fires in winter, chocolate, the view from the study window looking out over the Moray Firth and the Black Isle to the mountains beyond. And chocolate. I dislike driving on motorways, cooking, shopping, hospitals.

Acknowledgements

Thanks go to:

Allison Lane, whose course on English Architecture inspired me.

Shayne Rutherford of Darkmoon Graphics for the cover design.

My understanding husband: Jim Ross

Last, but definitely not least, my first reader: Amy Ross.

Sneak preview: Book 1 of Black Sheep: The Duke's Architect

FINSBURY SQUARE, LONDON; JANUARY

The Honourable Simon Payne pulled his shawl more tightly round his shoulders and glared balefully at the fire burning fitfully in the grate. It was not the fire's fault that it had so little power to heat the attic room. It was doing its best, he supposed, but there were limits to what could be expected of any fire against the freezing cold air trying to creep through even the smallest crack in the windows.

He sighed, remembering sorrowfully the brilliant blazes of his youth. There was no chill in any room at Edlesborough, no matter how frigid the outside air. But all that had changed fifteen years ago, when he had asked to be articled to an architect, and his father had stared at him as if he had two heads.

"*Articled?* To an *architect?* Nonsense! It is the army for you, my lad. That is the tradition for younger sons in the Payne family, since you are hardly suited to the church. John and Matthew are promising in that way, and will take up the two livings I have in my disposal, so you must go into the army. It will do you good — make a man of you, and none of this drawing nonsense. I can get you into the Guards, so you will not have to fight."

"No, sir."

"Good. That is settled. Next year, when you are sixteen, you will—"

"No, sir. I will not join the army."

His father's eyes had bulged like a frog's. "You will do as you are told!"

"No. Juliet said she will take care of me."

That brought on such an outpouring of rage that the physician had to be called, and Mama had brusquely packed Simon off to London to join Juliet at once.

And here he still was, still trying to become an architect, still failing miserably. Yet Juliet's small annuity managed to keep him in paper and pencils, and so he still designed his great houses in the Greek style, although he toyed with Gothick designs sometimes, too. But no one wanted them. They were much admired, but the men of wealth who could afford them preferred the established names like Stewart, Holland or Wyatt. How was a man ever to become an established name if no one would engage him? Just one house would make his reputation, he knew it.

Mary Ann brought him his afternoon pot of tea. It was weak, of course, since the leaves had to be reused and by supper were barely colouring the water, but at least it was hot and would warm him inside. He sipped gratefully, moving closer to the fire. Another quarter of an hour and he could add some more coals to it. Then there would be his glass of wine at dinner to look forward to.

He had barely begun his first cup of tea when Juliet dashed in, unwinding a voluminous scarf, her nose red from the cold.

Simon frowned. "Thought you intended to be out all morning."

"Indeed I was, but I called at the post office and there were *three* letters, which have been there for an age, the fellow said. Since Christmas, almost! Just imagine, and two are for you from your mama, so I brought them at once. Quick, quick, quick! How much is it?"

She tossed two small letters at him which he tried to catch but missed. Swiftly, Juliet bent down to pick them up. "Hurry up, Simon! The suspense is killing me."

He ripped open the first letter. "A hundred!" he said, awed, holding up half of a bank note. Tearing open the other, he held the two halves side by side. "A hundred pounds, sister! We can have beef steak for Sunday dinner."

"Or a turkey, perhaps," she murmured. "Or what do you say to a bit of partridge? I am so fond of partridge. And a box of those wonderful bonbons that Haydock's have."

"Let us not be too ambitious," he said, laughing. "We cannot say how long this will have to last us. It is six months, two weeks and three days since the last note, and that was only twenty."

"She must have had all the aunts and uncles at Edlesborough for Christmas," Juliet said. "You know how she does it — feed them up, pour Papa's best claret down their throats and then gently fleece them at the card table."

"It was only fifty after last Christmas," Simon said.

"So it was. She has had a successful time of it. I wish my mama were still alive, to send me little presents like this. Yours is very kind, and Papa knows nothing of it. The letters were not even franked, but I do not mind paying the postage when the contents are so rewarding."

"Three letters, you said. What was the other? A bill? We can settle for the coal now… and the butcher."

"Oh, yes. In all the excitement, I had forgotten." She fished the third letter from her reticule. "I do not recognise the hand. It is not a bill, I think." Breaking the seal, she unfolded it and read it silently, before looking up with a frown.

"What is it? Not bad news?"

"No… good news, I think, but… strange. Listen. *'To the Lady Juliet Payne, Finsbury Square, London. With humble greetings, my lady. You do not know me, but I am bidden to request you to bring Mr Simon Payne to Staineybank in Brinshire at your earliest convenience, in order to discuss the design for an orangery. Please reply directly to me to confirm your preferred date of travel, and I shall arrange private transportation and accommodation en route suitable to your station. Respectfully yours, A Goodenough (attorney at law), Castle Street, Brinchester'*. What do you think of that?"

"An orangery? Nothing else?"

"It is progress, Simon. Nothing but stables and kennels so far, so an orangery is a step up. A gentleman client, at least."

"But Mr Thwaite may yet settle on a design."

"Two years you have been working on designs for Mr Thwaite, and for all his great fortune, we have seen not a penny piece from it, nor has he actually commissioned any of your designs. But this… transport provided… a private carriage, Simon, just think! And suitable accommodation on the way. Oh, to be eating at someone else's expense! And when we arrive, we might even be invited to stay at the house itself. Staineybank… I have never heard of it."

"Campbell," Simon said. "English Palladian style. Built 1722."

She chuckled. "Yes, but who lives there?"

"Duke of Brinshire."

Her eyes widened. "A *duke!* Oh, Simon, we must go! Even if nothing comes of it, we must go."

"Yes," he said. "Campbell's houses are always worth seeing, and I have never seen that one. Of course we must go."

She shook her head, smiling. "You are incorrigible, brother. Very well, I shall write to this… what is his name? Mr Goodenough, attorney at law, and make arrangements, and you will be able to see Staineybank. And I… I shall endeavour to take as long as humanly possible to discuss this orangery in the hope that the duke will feed and house us both in the meantime. A fortnight, at least, surely, or even a whole month. And if he likes your designs, and who could not…" She shivered in anticipation. "Just think, Simon — we might see out the whole winter in comfort."

"And warmth," he said with feeling. "I hope Staineybank is warm."

***

STAINEYBANK, BRINSHIRE; JANUARY

Miss Sophia Merrington gazed at the image on the page before her and sighed. Such elegance! Such exquisite details! And, sadly, such extravagance. 'A light blue, or grey chemise robe, of gossamer net, imperial crape, or Spanish gauze, worn over white pealing satin, ornamented up the front with French bows and knots of silver', quoth the journal. White satin? Six shillings a yard at the very least, and possibly twice as much. The gauze would be a little less, and the bows and knots... she could make them quite small.

Then she read the next lines and despaired. ' A full melon sleeve, formed of the same material as the dress, and alternate stripes of white satin; finished with bows and knots of silver. A double roll of white satin round the neck of the robe, by way of tucker'. Full sleeves in stripes of two materials? A white satin tucker? And then the journal went on to describe the diamond comb in the hair, and diamonds for necklace, armlets and ear-rings.

She sighed even more heavily.

The slumbering figure on the sofa stirred. "Georgie? Oh, it is you, Sophia. Have I slept for a long time?"

"An hour or so, no more. Georgie went to see about the jellies. The duke came in to look at you, but I chased him away."

"He fusses so, but I am perfectly well. Just... tired. And enormous."

"Not much longer to wait now, Rowena," Sophia said briskly. She was very fond of her sister-in-law, and was delighted that Richard had married such a pleasant, unassuming woman, but the whole household revolved around her. If she should happen to fancy a certain dish at dinner, an army of gamekeepers and poultry maids and gardeners and still room maids would be mobilised to provide the ingredients. If she sneezed, the servants were thrown into a frenzy of possets and tisanes and tinctures, followed by a stream of midwives and apothecaries and physicians, who all recommended different remedies and stood in the hall roundly disparaging each other.

And the duke was the greatest worrier of them all. Since Richard was his official heir, the child Rowena carried would be the next in line, and oh, the hopes and expectations that rested on her to produce a son. Sophia could only hope for that, too, for then perhaps the trembling excitation that infected Staineybank would dissipate and they could all settle back into their usual activities. Not that there was much to look forward to in January, with the Christmas festivities past and not so much as an evening party on the horizon for months. It was dispiriting.

She sighed again.

Rowena heaved herself into a more upright position. "Now, what is making you sound so out of sorts? No ball to plan for, I imagine. What are you reading? Oh, this is pretty," she said, taking the journal from Sophia's hands. "White satin… French bows and knots of silver. That sounds quite delightful. Shall you have one like it made up?"

"I cannot afford it," Sophia said dejectedly.

"Not even with the additional allowance from the duke? He is very generous."

"Oh yes, the duke is generous, but Richard is not. I do not like to speak ill of my brother, for he is an admirable man in every other respect, but he is a nip-farthing, Rowena. Even you must admit it. He insists I must not overspend my allowance, not even by the cost of a single ribbon, and how can anyone be sure to keep to a specific sum? One must have clothes, after all."

"He is careful with money, it is true," Rowena said with a little smile. "Being a man, he does not quite appreciate the benefits of a new gown or slippers."

"Or diamond armlets," Sophia said with another sigh. "Just imagine how glorious that would be. With every movement, I should glimmer and sparkle."

She jumped up, held her arms in the correct position and executed a complete figure with all the steps, and then sighed again. "When, oh when will there be a ball? I cannot tell you, Rowena, how I long for a proper ball, but not when I have nothing to wear."

"There will be no balls before Lady Day when your next allowance will arrive, but perhaps the seamstress might begin work a little early? She will know she will be paid, after all."

"Richard will not permit it," Sophia said dejectedly. "We are never to buy anything for which we could not settle the bill immediately, if required. Nor are we allowed to borrow money, and we are never, ever to gamble to defray debts. Oh, it is hard! There is nothing like a new ball gown to lift the spirits."

"Then you know the answer, Sophia," Rowena said with a quick laugh. "You will just have to marry a vastly rich man who dotes on you so much that he gives you all his wealth to spend on ball gowns and diamond armlets."

"All his wealth? But then we should be destitute and how should I survive without any new gowns at all?"

Rowena laughed out loud at her dejected tone. "There is no pleasing you! What you must do, Sophia, is what I was obliged to do for many years, and rework your old gowns. You have some very pretty ones that could be refreshed with very little effort."

It was a strange thing, but Richard had said precisely the same thing to her many, many times, and it had merely made her cross and long even harder for the new gown or gloves or fan. When Rowena said it, however, it sounded eminently reasonable and she could not think of a single argument against it.

Richard himself came in just then, with his sketchbook under his arm, and Sophia had no wish to hear any more about his precious orangery. For months now, he had been drawing up plans for it, so that Rowena might grow oranges and lemons and who knows what exotic fruits, and Sophia was tired of it.

Leaving them to their discussion, she slipped away to her room, and flung open the doors of the two presses that housed all her ball gowns. She had quite a collection now after eleven years of balls and she had bought at least two for each season. Laying them carefully on the bed, she counted thirty-one. Since each gown had danced its way through four or five balls apiece, that was... too difficult a sum to work in her head. She kept a notebook with every ball listed, and all her partners, and what they had danced, together with a few comments about the number of couples and the quality of the supper and any particularly memorable moments, so she could work it out from that.

After some concentrated effort with the notebook, she reached a final number — one hundred and forty-one. That was the sum of her life so far, one hundred and forty-one balls, any number of dances and partners and not a single offer of marriage. Even in the days of her highest bloom she had attracted no suitors, and now, at the advanced age of twenty-eight, it was unlikely that she ever would. She was a confirmed spinster, and even three older sisters in the same pitiable state was no comfort. What was wrong with them all, that no man wanted any of them?

She lifted up her favourite gown, her very first. Horribly outdated now, of course — such full skirts! So much material in it, and even Richard had agreed that she must wear silk to a ball. She pressed the fabric to her face, wondering if she would still catch the faint scent of the perfume she had worn on that unforgettable evening... No, it was gone.

With another sigh, she carried it to the window to examine more closely. Such a beautiful silk, that flowed over her hands like cool water. And so much of it... if it could be carefully unpicked, perhaps a new dress could be contrived? And there would even be enough left over for full sleeves, if she should want them.

Gathering up the gown, she rushed off to find Lily. The duchess was almost the same age as Sophia, and also came from a family at the lower edge of gentility, where finding the money for new gowns was a constant struggle. Even since her marriage to the duke, she still dressed frugally, and was adept at fashioning new from old.

"Have you never had to do this before?" Lily said, taking the gown to the window to examine it closely. "Richard must have been very generous with you."

"Not he!" Sophia said. "The trustees were generous, certainly, but as soon as Richard came of age, he leased Leahollow and marched us off to a poky little house in Norwich, and reduced our allowances."

"Oh!" Lily said, wide-eyed. "But perhaps there were debts to be settled?"

"No, he is just horridly cheeseparing. It is not so bad for my sisters, for Charlotte is as tight-fisted as Richard, Augusta is happy so long as she has a riding habit to wear, and Maria cares nothing for clothes when there are books to be read. Mama was the only one who understood, but even she could not sway Richard. His mind was entirely closed to the idea that one cannot exist on only two or three gowns a year. It is just not possible, not if one is to be respectably turned out."

Lily laughed. "Indeed, I cannot fault your logic, cousin, for my sisters and I suffered just as you do. Poor Papa! There were so many of us, and the boys had to be educated and mounted, so there was very little left over for unnecessary items like clothing. We were only allowed new gowns twice a year, spring and autumn, and then it was only one morning gown, one walking and one evening. We spent half our days unpicking and sewing anew."

"How dreadful!"

"Oh, it was a challenge we all relished. Happily for me, my godmother descended on us when I was about to come out, and insisted I needed a veritable mountain of gowns. Papa grumbled about it, and we only persuaded him in the end by telling him that good quality clothes could be handed down for year after year, and serve for several of my sisters."

"I imagine he did not grumble so much when you drew the duke's eye," Sophia said slyly.

"Oh, but he did! He was horrified, and I think he would have forbidden the match if Mama and my godmother had not pointed out all the advantages. And now Cordelia and Amabel have made very good matches, and John has his colours, in a far better regiment than he might have expected, and Henry is a midshipman. There is a living for Charles or Thomas, too, if they want to go into the church. The duke has been so kind to us... to all of us," she added wistfully.

Sophia said nothing, for she found Lily's story heartbreaking. To be forced to marry a man old enough to be one's grandfather! Lily had been eighteen to the duke's sixty-eight, and no matter how kind he had been and still was, for he was clearly fond of his young wife, it was indubitably a dreadfully unequal match. As for the advantages, those all accrued to others — Lily's brothers and sisters, and not to Lily herself, beyond the security of wealth and high standing in society.

But Lily never railed at her situation, except to say now and then that the grandeur and size of Staineybank felt oppressive to her. After her only child had died at the age of six, she had planned to leave it altogether and return to Cheshire, where her family lived, but here she still was.

Now she smiled, running slender fingers over the skirts of the ballgown. "This is a beautiful silk. It will make up afresh very well, you will see. We can look through the journals today, and talk to the seamstress tomorrow."

The two spent a delightful afternoon in the duchess's private sitting room, with journals lying open on every available surface, sipping tea and discussing fashions, for it was a subject of inexhaustible interest to both of them.

Dinner that evening was dominated as so often these days by discussion of the proposed orangery. It was intended as a wedding gift to Rowena, who had admired the Duke of Camberley's orangery at Marshfields, but at the present rate of progress the bride would be a matron with three or four children before it was finished. Not a stone had yet been laid, and the exact location had not even been determined.

As always with Richard, it came down to money. The duke was all for a grandiose scheme on a hill to impress visitors, lined with marble pillars. Richard was more inclined for a simple brick structure, on account of the cost of glass, and as for marble, it was not to be thought of. No matter how many times the duke pointed out that he would be paying for it and the estate could easily bear the cost and it would be a gratifying celebration of the birth of the next heir, it made no difference.

Sophia was glad to creep away to bed and dream of balls and the swirl of silken gowns, of rooms filled with waving feathers and sparkling jewels, and everywhere music and charming young men eager to dance. And surely there would be one, just one, who would look at her and truly see her.

***

The next morning, she awoke to steady snow, coating the gardens in white icing. By breakfast, the fall was reduced to a few stray flakes, but there was a flurry of activity amongst the men, anxiously discussing the roads, while most of the ladies had wisely decided to take breakfast in bed.

"Let us escape," Lily whispered to Sophia. "The seamstress will not be able to get up from the village today, but there is much we can do. I thought we might look at the rest of your gowns and see what else might be reworked."

Sophia could see no flaw in this enticing plan, so they left the men muttering about oxen and sweepers, and crept away to Sophia's room.

She was still unused to an entire room all to herself, having shared with Mary all her life. At first, she had confined her things to the accustomed half of the room, leaving ample space for Mary's piles of books, but she had soon realised the luxury of taking up every inch of space herself, if she wanted it. Not that she did. Oddly, the more space she had to fill, the less she wanted to clutter up every surface with abandoned bits and pieces. Only a few small ornaments, symmetrically positioned, graced the mantelpiece, her hairbrushes sat in a neat arrangement on her dressing table, a single journal lay on the bedside table in case she should be wakeful at night and everything else was hidden away in drawers and cupboards.

In under an hour, Lily had selected seven gowns that could readily be converted to a more fashionable style. Only two were ball gowns and one an evening gown, but Sophia could not deny that four new morning gowns would be very welcome, too. Their two lady's maids were summoned to give their advice, a pot of tea brought and all was going on in the most satisfactory manner when Spearman, the butler, came in.

"Beg pardon, Your Grace, Miss Merrington, but there's a Lady Juliet Payne and Mr Simon Payne just arrived."

Lily's face registered bewilderment. "I do not know them. Sophia, do you? No? Are they perhaps acquaintances of the duke, Spearman?"

"Not that I'm aware, Your Grace."

"Perhaps they are stranded by the snow... a carriage breakdown," Sophia suggested.

"I don't think so, madam," the butler said. "They seem to think they're expected... something to do with the plans for the orangery."

"Then Mr Richard Merrington must have invited them," Lily said.

"Oh, yes, of course," Spearman said, brightening. "That will be it, and I dare say he forgot to mention it, what with the snow and all. It's a pity he's out with the oxen team just now. I'll let Miss Hester know. She can arrange rooms and deal with them."

"Oh, no, indeed, I must receive them myself," Lily said at once. "As a noblewoman, Lady Juliet will expect it."

The two visitors stood rather forlornly in the Marble Hall, their luggage in a puddly heap near the door, while an assortment of servants awaited instructions. Mr Payne was gazing around the Marble Hall with its array of pillars reaching imperiously to the high ceiling, his expression of awe one that Sophia entirely understood. She had never quite accustomed herself to the grandeur of Staineybank herself. Lady Juliet, oddly, was engaged in watching Mr Payne.

They were a strange couple. Lady Juliet was tiny, a doll-like figure of around forty, while Mr Payne, perhaps ten years younger, was a large man in every sense, both tall and broad of chest, and as handsome a man as Sophia had ever seen. No... that was not quite true, for there had been a man of ethereal beauty at her very first ball, but he had not even noticed her and she had never seen him again. Nevertheless, he remained an ideal of manhood, but she suspected that Mr Simon Payne, once unwrapped from the many layers of his winter travelling garments, might come very close.

"Lady Juliet, welcome to Staineybank," Lily said. "I am the Duchess of Brinshire."

It was, perhaps, an unnecessary introduction, for the flurry of bows and curtsies from the assembled servants must have suggested her rank, but Lady Juliet turned to her in some surprise.

"Oh! Duchess! I had not expected..." Only then, rather belatedly, did she drop into her own curtsy.

"You are here to see Mr Richard Merrington, I understand?" Lily said brightly.

"Well... I am not sure..."

"It is about the orangery, is it not? Then that is his project."

"Is it? I did not know that," she said vaguely. Then, in a sharper tone, "Simon, do not wander away when her grace is speaking."

"But it is a perfect cube," he said, his face alight with inner fire. "And the pillars... Corinthian, and the frieze is so elegant. Do you not think?"

"Well, I am sure, but do please pay attention when her grace is addressing you."

He turned puzzled eyes on her. "I am complimenting her house, Juliet. She cannot object to that, can she?"

Lady Juliet sighed, but Lily only laughed. "Actually, Mr Payne, I am very pleased that you admire Staineybank, but I find it oppressively grandiose myself."

"Oh no," he said solemnly. "It is beautiful. Campbell, you see. Wonderful architect."

"I am sure he was," Lily said diplomatically. "But if you are not here at Mr Richard Merrington's behest, who was it who invited you?"

"Goodenough," Mr Payne said. "Attorney. Brinchester."

"Mr Goodenough!" Sophia cried. "But there is no such person!"

"I assure you there is," Lady Juliet said robustly. "He wrote to us and then brought us here himself from London in the most commodious style. The carriage is still outside, awaiting our instructions."

"I am afraid it is quite true," Lily said. "Mrs Richard Merrington arrived here last year in precisely the same manner — a letter from a person calling himself Goodenough, who brought her here, whereupon he disappeared. There is no attorney in Brinchester by that name."

Lady Juliet turned and almost ran across the Marble Hall, wrenched open the door before the footman could reach it and raced outside. The others followed more slowly, knowing what she would find.

The drive was empty, only the twin tracks in the snow betraying that a carriage had arrived and had now left, making its way down the drive and not to the Staineybank stables.

"Then it is true," Lady Juliet said. "We have been duped. But why? Why would anyone play such a cruel trick on us?"

But no one had an answer to offer.

END OF SAMPLE CHAPTER of *The Duke's Architect*; for more information or to buy, go to at my website at https://marykingswood.co.uk.

Printed in Dunstable, United Kingdom

76628658R10119